DRACULA BEYOND STOKER

Issue 4.5

DBS Press

Dracula Beyond Stoker
Issue 4.5

Tucker Christine
editor

Edward G. Pettit
consulting editor

Published by DBS Press
ISBN - 978-1-963391-04-6 (Paperback)
ISBN - 978-1-963391-05-3 (e-book)
August, 2024

www.dbspress.com
www.draculabeyondstoker.com

Letter From the Editor to the Reader

31 July

Friends,

I must admit this issue got away from me a little bit.

I always knew that the half issue following the *Brides* was going to include Wayne Rogers's "Dracula's Brides," a weird, wild, and wonderful pulp novelette from 1941 that really has nothing to do with Stoker's monster but doesn't exist without him. What I didn't know was what, if anything, would accompany it.

And then I was presented with an overabundance of fantastic tales for Issue 4. That became the longest of the main issues so far, but I still had more that I wanted to publish, so I'm giving them to you here—in the longest of the half issues.

Kay Hanifen returns to our pages with "A Guest for Dinner," in which the count enlists a village girl to help him prepare for the arrival of a certain Englishman, much to the consternation of his *two* brides. Jamie Flanagan presents an epistolary dialog between Dracula and his brides regarding that same visitor in "The Solicitor." And Michael R. Colangelo bridges our gap between issues 4 and 5 in the beautiful and gruesome "Brides."

I'm off to read stories of Jack, Arthur, and Quincey so as to provide you with another great book in November.

Until then,
Best,
Tucker

A Guest for Dinner
By Kay Hanifen

Dracula's Diary
(Translated from Medieval Romanian)

19 April

I have received word that my solicitor is arriving from London soon, so I must prepare my home. He is like a fly, and I am a spider. If I spin my web correctly, he won't realize that he's ensnared until I've sunk my fangs into him.

It's strange. I have decomposed in this castle for so long that I've forgotten how humanity lives. Over the past week, I've ventured to the village and watched them converse, prepare their meals, and complete their chores. It's like watching cattle interact in the field and making notes of when they graze and when they're milked and when they're put to work plowing and sowing. I realize now how much work I must do to make this place pass for a home belonging to the living.

There was a recipe I remembered enjoying when I lived. Pomegranate Chicken was rather simple and flavorful. I attempted it tonight, much to the amusement of my brides who do not understand why I must leave this crypt. For centuries, blood has tasted sweeter than wine, and I've desired nothing else, but tonight, I found myself looking forward to tasting human food once more.

I must have recreated the recipe incorrectly because it smelled burned and the sauce had somehow curdled. I knew that it would not be fit for even the most desperate peasant to eat. I shall make the attempt again tomorrow night.

20 April

I made the recipe correctly tonight. Of this I am certain. It looked and smelled exactly as I remembered. Even my brides were drawn to the kitchen to see what I had created.

My elder bride, Erzsebet, watched as I plated it with salad and a slice of bread that I had stolen from the bakery. "I am impressed. That almost looks appetizing," she said.

"Well, you've left me to play host all by myself," I replied, taking a seat at my dining room table, the way I did when I was alive, and slicing into the tender flesh of the chicken. Spearing it with my fork—I've heard they're now fashionable to use, unlike in my lifetime—I studied it to ensure that it was not pink in the middle and watched idly as the dark juice slid off it.

"Are you going to watch or are you going to try it?" my younger bride, Mariska, asked.

Erzsebet slapped her upside the head. "Show some respect for the Master."

She studied her feet. "Forgive me, master."

"Already forgotten." Without any further preamble, I shoved it into my mouth.

And I regretted it the moment that vile thing passed my lips. It tasted like rot and decay, which should be impossible because I killed the chicken myself earlier tonight and all my other ingredients were almost equally fresh. I spat it out.

"I suppose looks are deceiving," Erzsebet remarked.

A wave of frustration and anger swelled inside me, and I swept the plate off the table. It shattered, making my brides wince. "I don't understand. I did it correctly this time."

"Perhaps the problem lies not in your skills but in your tongue," Mariska suggested.

I turned my ire upon her. "What, pray tell, does that mean?"

She met my gaze unflinchingly. "Simply that the food of the living is not meant for us anymore, Master. Perhaps you need a human subject to experiment upon first."

To my surprise, she made an excellent point. I had been so wrapped up in reconnecting with my former humanity that I had forgotten what set me apart and made me superior. "Very well. I will find a human to feed rather than feed upon."

21 April

Though the local villagers are wary of me, they also have far too few resources and far too many mouths to feed. It is not so difficult to trade gold for a farmer's daughter or an unwanted newborn. I make sure to reward them according to their usefulness.

Tonight, I took the carriage to a decrepit farm, carrying with me a sizeable dowry. In my observations over the course of the week, I came to the conclusion that the girl who lived here was a rose amid dry brush. If she were a man, she might have found her fortune in the city, but alas, she was cursed to live out her days like all women, working the fields and acting as her husband's broodmare. At least, this would be her fate had I not intervened.

I knocked on the door to the hovel. On the inside, I could hear a baby crying, children laughing, and the slurred recriminations of their presumably drunk father. The girl opened the door. When she recognized me, she opened her mouth to scream, but I already held her in my gaze. "Silence, child," I commanded, and she was. I handed her the gold. "Give this to your father. You belong to me now."

"Who the hell are you?" he demanded before she could obey my orders.

"I am here to collect your daughter," I said, using my powers over the feeble human mind against him, "I have left you a considerable dowry."

He gave a stiff bow. "Yes, my lord. Of course."

"Come, child," I beckoned, and she followed wordlessly. I opened the door to the carriage for her, and she hesitated, clearly fighting the will I exerted over her. I would be impressed if it wasn't so inconvenient. "Get into the carriage."

She moved with hesitating, faltering steps and I couldn't help my smile. The girl was going to be a fascinating experiment. Once she was situated and I was in the driver's seat, I flicked the reins and set the horses to a brisk canter.

"You may speak now," I said.

"What do you want from me?"

Looking over my shoulder, I flashed her a grin. "I want to have you for dinner. If you do everything as I say, I will let you go free, but if you disobey me, you'll suffer the consequences."

She gulped, and the rabbiting rhythm of her heart made my mouth water. Fear always sweetens the prey, in my opinion, and I suspected that her blood would be like a fine wine in this state.

"Tell me your name," I commanded.

She replied, "Kitarni." Shrinking in on herself, she asked, "Why me?"

I shrugged. "I thought you would make a good company for dinner."

When we reached the castle, I bade her to stay in the dining room until I was ready. Erzsebet and Mariska stood guard, hovering behind her as I prepared the pomegranate chicken. I knew they thirsted for the young blood, but I needed her first.

After plating the meal, I set it in front of her with a knife, fork, and glass of wine. She looked up at me in confusion. "I don't understand."

"What is there to not understand? How a knife and fork work?"

"You said you wanted to have me for dinner."

"Yes, you're here, and you're having dinner. I would eat, but I have certain dietary restrictions. I want you to tell me what you truly think of this meal. Do not try to spare my feelings."

She lifted the knife and fork with shaking hands before slicing into it the chicken. Chewing thoughtfully, she said, "It tastes good, I suppose, but the chicken is a little dry."

"A little dry?" I repeated as my two wives giggled behind me.

She nodded warily and speared the roasted potato I had elected to use to compliment the sauce. "And the roasted potatoes are a little underdone." Slicing into the chicken once more, she took another bite. "It's not terrible, though."

"Not terrible," Erzsebet tittered, "I would call that damnation by faint praise if we weren't damned to begin with."

Kitarni blanched but wisely said nothing.

"How would you suggest I ensure that the chicken is not dry, and the potatoes are thoroughly cooked?" I asked.

"For the chicken, you must cover it for a time while cooking, and for the potatoes, you must spear them with a fork." She sat ramrod straight and eyes downcast to study her hands in her lap.

I nodded to myself. "Thank you, Kitarni. You are dismissed. Mariska, show her to where she may rest for the day. I cleaned and aired out the blue room last night."

"Yes, Master," she replied, grabbing the girl by the shoulder and half dragging her away.

Erzsebet watched her disappear down the hall before saying, "She is a pretty young rose, isn't she?"

"Oh really? I hadn't noticed."

She scoffed. "Vladimir, I've known you for centuries, and you have all the fidelity of Zeus. With a beauty like that, you'll want to pluck and preserve her before she can wilt in a few short years."

"Perhaps, but I have other concerns." As if to illustrate my point, I heard a shriek from the other room. We ran towards the noise and found Mariska with her teeth sunk deep into Kitarni's throat. The girl was ashen faced, her eyes rolled back in a swoon. I grabbed my wife by the scruff of the neck like a misbehaving kitten and pulled her off the girl. Erzsebet caught her before she fell.

"What on earth were you thinking?" I demanded.

Her eyes brimmed with bloody tears. "I'm hungry, Master. It's been more than a week since we've hunted, and my throat burns."

Had it really been that long? I knew I was wrapped up in my preparations, but perhaps I have not been the most attentive husband. I dropped her to the ground. "Tomorrow," I said, "I shall bring you something to feed upon tomorrow."

Erzsebet returned moments later looking irritated. "She's resting." Turning to Mariska, she said, "You're a fool, girl, to defy your master's orders and risk his preparations. You deserve nothing."

I raised a placating hand. "It is all right, Erzsebet. I know you must be thirsty too, and I apologize for ignoring your needs."

Tomorrow, I shall go into the village and steal away a child. They are unwary creatures, and I can easily lure one into my thrall. It should be enough to sustain me and my brides for some time.

22 April

I retrieved a small boy from a nearby orphanage. He will not be missed by anyone and will sate our thirst for a while. The blood of the innocent is the finest delicacy we can enjoy. He wiggled and fought the sack I placed him in until I commanded him to sleep. He slept the whole journey home.

After drinking my fill, I left him in my brides' room and returned to the kitchen. Kitarni woke soon after, and I prepared her the same meal as the night before, but with her advice taken to heart. When she took a bite, she smiled. "This is excellent."

I couldn't help my own smile as she finished her plate. "Wonderful. You are dismissed."

She blinked in confusion. "Is that all?"

"Yes, until your mid-evening meal."

"I don't understand why you're doing this. Are you trying to fatten me up for the slaughter or…"

There was no harm in telling her the truth. "I have a guest coming in a little more than a week's time, and I must make it appear as though this castle is full of life. I cannot taste what I make, and he cannot know what I truly am."

"And you're practicing your cooking skills on me." She gnawed her lip thoughtfully. "I can teach you how to cook, clean, and make this place appear fully staffed, if you would like."

Taken aback, I said, "I would love nothing more, Madame Kitarni."

The rest of the day was spent teaching me how to beat out dust filled blankets, scrub floors, wash dishes, and dust tables and shelves. I must say that Kitarni brought some new light to this dreary place. She'd sing bawdy songs while she worked or tell quaint stories of her life on the farm.

Midnight meal was pork, which she admonished for being undercooked (I had forgotten the many kinds of diseases you can contract after eating the wrong type of meat). Apparently, I also went a little too heavy on the rosemary with the bread, but they were otherwise delicious.

Taking a sip of wine from her glass, she asked, "What is it like?"

"I am not sure what you mean, my dear."

"Immortality at the expense of others."

"What is on your plate?" I asked.

She blinked. "Pork, bread, and greens, but I don't see how —"

"Were they alive, once?"

"Yes."

"And what would happen if I denied you these once living things?"

She paled slightly but kept an admirable nerve in the face of something easily construed as a threat. "I would die."

I smiled, revealing my fangs. "So, you too survive at the expense of other living beings. Oh, but you say I kill the innocent. Well, what crime had the chicken and the swine committed against you? The cabbage and the potatoes are without sin, are they not? We all survive by eating the weak."

"If it's so natural, why are you repulsed by holy images and crucifixes?" she asked.

"Perhaps for the same reason that you are repulsed by the unholy and fire is repulsed by water. We are simply opposites."

She opened her mouth to argue and then closed it, her brows furrowed. And then, to my surprise, the girl smirked. "Well, I suppose that having grown up on a farm, I can attest to the evils committed by chickens and pigs. They'll eat anything without remorse."

I raised my eyebrows, unable to control the smile growing on my face. "Is that so?"

She nodded. "One of our neighbors, an old man, fell in his pig pen. As he struggled to get up, they devoured him. They tore him apart so thoroughly that his own wife and brother barely recognized his corpse."

"Death by swine would be an embarrassing way to go," I replied with a laugh.

She shrugged. "Fair is fair, I suppose. He eats pork for years, so it's only natural that they should be allowed a taste of their master's flesh. He was a cruel man, anyway. His wife always came to town with black eyes and a limp." Kitarni leaned in close. "Between you and me, I suspect that he didn't so much fall as be pushed. His wife married the brother a month later, and from what I hear, they're quite happy."

"You approve of this murder?" I asked, unable to contain my surprise. "Doesn't your holy book condemn it?"

The gaze she held with me was bold and ferocious, reminding me of a lioness or a wolf. "It was self-defense after years of suffering. She earned her freedom from his fists and his rank breath and wandering hands. God once ordered the deaths of all people in Jericho, including innocent women and children. I'm sure He'll understand this transgression by a desperate old woman."

"Perhaps," I acquiesced, "In my time, I've discovered that there are plenty of exceptions and justifications for even the most mortal of sins."

She swirled the wine in her glass and flashed me a charming smile. "What is it like being immortal, then?"

"Surprisingly dull after a point," I replied. "I've fought many a war and travelled to the ends of the earth before growing homesick and returning to my beloved Wallachia. After a rather dull century, I hear that the world is progressing with new wonders, and I wish to see for myself if it's become more interesting in my absence."

"Is it lonely?"

"Yes," I replied, surprised by my own candor, "In life, Erzsebet and Mariska were once close companions. I admired my first wife, Erzsebet, for her strength and power. In my time, I was known as a brutal warlord, but her thirst for blood would often outdo my own. But there was another side to her, a side of wit and righteous fury that I truly admired. My second wife, Mariska, was a clever girl, much like you, and I valued her incisive wisdom. Erzsebet saw the monster in me and fell in love with it. Mariska saw the man and fell in love with him. All that changed, though, when I turned them. I suspect that a vampiric transformation caused them to lose a part of their soul. Erzsebet's righteous fury became a sadism that I cannot control, and a wall of ice has formed between me and Mariska. I hope that I might find someone in England whose soul can survive the transformation."

"I miss my mother and father," she admitted while studying her plate. "My siblings too. Our house was small, and Papa enjoyed the drink a bit too much for any of our liking, but it was a home, and our family is full of love and laughter."

She looked so despondent that I briefly considered allowing her to return home but decided that it was best for her to stay here. At home, she was fated for a brief and hard life, but here, if she pleased me, I could grant her greater eternal life than God Himself. Instead of rising to her bait, I picked up her plate and whisked it away to the kitchen.

In a few short nights, my solicitor will be here, and I need to decide if I want to keep her or let my wives devour her. On the one hand, I enjoyed her companionship and would like for it to continue. On the other, I am leaving very soon, and I have no desire to bring anyone with me. Is now truly the right time to create another bride? Newborn vampires require a lot of patience and fresh blood. I will be unable to provide those things while also preparing for my journey. But I want her, so I must have her as soon as I've perfected my cooking skills. Until then, I shall add an extra ingredient to the wine for her to drink.

Her final meal for the evening was my second attempt at the pork. This time, it was perfect…except for one thing.

"Do you know what would make this recipe much better? A bit of garlic. And then your guest will love it."

I hissed. "There is no garlic in this castle."

At that, she tilted her head like a confused puppy. "Why not?"

"It's revolting," I replied. "Now eat your dinner."

She nodded and returned to her meal. For a moment, I thought that I would have to be the one that began the conversation again, but she said, "Is there anything you fear? With powers like yours, I cannot imagine fearing anything."

I shook my head, partly because it was the truth and partly because I suspected why she asked me that question, and it filled me with disappointment. I had hoped she would be cleverer than this. "I fear what happens after death. I know that I'm not a good man, and I never tried to be, so there is only one place I shall go. But I also fear centuries alone, with no one to love." I sighed, shaking my head, and adding a half-truth for her to do with it what she would. "Before I transformed, I feared that I would never see the sun again. Once I became a creature of the night, I feared the daylight, for I will burn to ash if I step into the sun again."

Picking at her food, she said, "I fear bites and the infection that comes from them. When I was a child, my brother was bitten by a mad dog, and then he changed. He became twitchy, aggressive, saw things that weren't there, and could not eat or drink near the end. He died seizing and in a pool of his own drool."

"That is an awful way to go," I replied.

Looking up demurely from her plate, she said, "To me, there are fates worse than death." She took a sip of her wine. Setting down the goblet, she squinted at it as though it was a puzzle to be solved.

"Is everything all right?" I asked.

"It tastes different."

I flashed her a smile. "Ah, yes, that. I am impressed by your palate. It is true that the wine is different. I ran out of my fine Greek wine and dug out a bottle of Amontillado from Spain. I thought it was a rather good vintage. Is it not to your liking?"

"It's wonderful," she replied, draining the glass and then yawning. "All these late nights have left me rather tired. I think I shall get some rest."

I waved genially. "Good day, Kitarni."

"Good day, Count Dracula," she replied and disappeared into her room.

I sensed the presence of my second wife before I saw her. Without looking up from clearing the table, I said, "What is it, Mariska?"

She emerged from the shadows, her green eyes piercing. "The girl intends to betray you. She'll be the death of us all."

"Darling, we are already dead." Not wanting to bother with the dirty dishes, I simply tossed them out the window. I had enough plates to feed an army; losing a few would mean nothing to me.

She crossed her arms like a put-out child on the verge of a tantrum. "You know that is not what I'm saying."

"Yes, the same way that I know she cannot kill me. She can try, but many have tried over the centuries. I won't be defeated by a woman so young that she might as well be in diapers."

"But—" she began, but I cut her off.

"Are you questioning your master's authority? Or are you questioning his power?"

Averting her eyes, she replied, "No, Master. I am simply concerned."

I squeezed her shoulder affectionately. "I hear you, but you must trust in me. She's nothing."

27 April

I've been a fool. When she did not make an attempt on my life on the first day or the second, I assumed that she faltered in her plans or abandoned them altogether. I did not expect to awaken in my coffin with my arms and legs burning because she had bound my hands and feet with rosaries. My wives' coffins were covered in garlic and wild roses to keep them at bay while she stood over me with a wooden stake and hammer. She was framed by sunlight like an angel of God's vengeance.

"What are you doing, little girl?" I growled.

"Fair is fair. The farmer kills the lowly swine until one day, he is caught unaware, and the swine kills the farmer. I shall rid the world of your evil or die trying rather than become your meal or your brides'."

I must say, a part of me was impressed. It was foolish of me to allow her so close to my heart, but like a true warrior, she used it to her advantage. Most humans cower at the sight of me and blindly obey lest they face my wrath. This was the first true challenge I've faced in centuries.

Holding the stake to my chest with one hand, she raised the hammer with the other. With my hands still bound, I grabbed her wrist and flung her into a wall. The holy items weakened me, but not enough. I heard the crunch of bone snapping as she landed, and ignoring the way it burned, I liberated myself from the rosaries.

Kitarni was crawling away, one of her arms bent at an unnatural angle. Though a part of me admired her, another, greater part raged at the fact that this woman—this girl—caught me unawares and humiliated me. I kicked her in the stomach, grinning in satisfaction as her ribs cracked and she slammed into the wall, leaving fissures on impact.

She lay there choking, her blood gushing from her throat and pouring out her mouth. I kissed her, drinking deeply of her sweet lifeblood before returning to the coffins of my brides and brushing away the flowers and garlic. Throwing open their lids, I announced, "My brides, it is time to feast."

They shot from their coffins like hunting dogs released to catch a fox. I watched them drain her for a moment before grabbing the rosaries with a kerchief and flinging them out the window.

But I suppose I wasn't done being made to look the fool, because as soon as my brides had their fill, Kitarni shot up with a gasp. I had forgotten that I'd been feeding her my blood. I thought that perhaps because she could handle the things that can hurt us, the infection hadn't taken hold. Apparently, I was wrong.

Grabbing the discarded stake and hammer, I approached. I decided I would make an example of her to my brides. This is what happens when you betray me. But then her eyes filled with tears, and she cried, "Forgive me, Master. I did not understand before, but now I do. I was a fool, and now I am eager to obey."

"Kill her," Mariska said. "We cannot trust a word out of her mouth."

Erzsebet's lips twitched as she fought expressing her amusement on her face. "I don't know about you, Vladimir, but she is the most interesting thing to happen in ages. It would be a shame to throw away such a lovely new toy."

She had a point. Kitarni had been the biggest challenge I've faced since the crusades. "Very well," I said, tossing the weapons aside, "a test, then. Kitarni, do you wish to do whatever your master wishes?"

"Yes," she breathed without hesitation.

"Get to your feet," I commanded, and she obeyed. "Bow to the three of us and then strip to your underclothes." Once again, she did as I asked. The girl was entirely beholden to my will. I do not know why that disappoints me so.

Erzsebet and Mariska have taken her out hunting. The first kill is always the most exciting, and I had no desire to infringe upon this, especially if it meant peace among my brides.

In my preparations for the solicitor, I realize that Kitarni has taught me much about being human. I know now that I gave her too much freedom, and it led only to more defiance. I shall have to restrict my guest's movements about the castle if I have any hope of maintaining the ruse. Perhaps most importantly, I learned to never underestimate humanity. When they want to, they can be cunning beyond their years, so I must not let my guard down as the fly enters the spider's web. I shall wait patiently for the arrival of the solicitor, and the fun can truly begin.

Kay Hanifen was born on a Friday the 13th and once lived for three months in a haunted castle. So, obviously, she had to become a horror writer. Her articles have appeared in Ghouls Magazine, Screen Rant, The Borgen Project, and Leatherneck magazine; and her short stories have appeared in Strangely Funny VIII, Crunchy With Ketchup, Dark Shadows: The Gay Nineties, Wicked Newsletters, Fearful Fun, Death of a Bad Neighbor, Enchanted Entrapments, Diet Riot: A Fatterpunk Anthology, M is for Medical, Blood Moon, Terror in the Trenches, Slice of Paradise, Vinyl Cuts, Sherlock Holmes and Watson's Medical Mysteries, Beware the Bugs, Rockets and Robots, Divergent Terror, and Devil's Rejects. When she's not consuming pop culture with the voraciousness of a vampire at a 24-hour blood bank, you can usually find her with her two black cats or at kayhanifenauthor.wordpress.com.

Dracula's Brides
By Wayne Rogers

Chapter 1.
The Pampered Corpse

Murder! All week, Jim Hanley had been steeped to the ears in crime. Every newspaper had been frantically shouting "Crime Wave." Wherever he turned, fresh details of the barbarous Reign of Terror that was spreading over New York had confronted him. Resolutely, he had reminded himself that he was a private investigator, the depredations of the savage "Wolf Pack" were police business and not his—but he was like a chained hound with the game prowling all around him.

Robbery and wanton murder always stirred his blood and meet him itch to come to grips with the perpetrators. And these murders were deliberately wanton. Not satisfied with highly successful robbery, rich looting such as New York had seldom seen, the thieves had butchered watchmen, guards, policeman, as if a hunger-mad pack of wolves had pounced upon them....

When the Crissmans had invited him to spend the weekend in somnolent Yorktown Heights, the midwinter quiet of rural Westchester County had appealed to him irresistibly. That would be a respite, a two day escape from omnipresent crime, he had told himself as he accepted—and now, on a peaceful Sunday afternoon, one of the restless house-party guests proposed that they play "Murder!" And the rest chimed in with enthusiastic agreement.

"OK," the organizer promptly took charge. "Let's have a deck of cards, and we'll draw to see who will be the corpse. Come on— gather 'round."

Hanley groaned inwardly. His gray eyes were wearily protesting as he lifted his blond head from the comfortable pillow of an easy chair, and heaved his big body upright. Now they had to have a corpse—

But before they had finished drawing cards fate stepped in—to provide a corpse ready-made! Suddenly the side door flung open, and young Bud Crissman came running into the room. Wild-eyed with excitement, he stopped in the doorway, panting for breath.

"Dad—Happy Harry—he has a dead woman—in the Mc-Kinnon house!" He gasped. "I saw him going in—I crept up after him and saw her—upstairs in bed! She looked awful—and he's talking to her—talking to her and trying to make her eat!"

Happy Harry was a harmless half-wit, a man of thirty-five or forty with the brain of a child. Hanley and most of the others had seen him the day before when he came shambling along Baptist Church Road, grinning and talking to himself. Happy Harry, feeding a corpse! Startled eyes turned to the ten-year-old, but his father took Bud in charge, gradually calmed him, and elicited a more lucid account.

The Theodore McKinnon place, half a mile down the road, had been closed in the fall, and would not be reopened until spring. Bud, it seemed, had noticed the half-wit prowling around the grounds, and had gone closer to see what he was up to. He had seen Harry surreptitiously enter the back door of the building. When he did not reappear, Bud had climbed a tree, from which he could peer into the back rooms of the upper floor—and had been astounded to see the fellow sitting beside a bed solicitously tending his ghastly patient.

"She was *dead*—I could see that plain," he repeated in wide-eyed awe. "She just lay there, and didn't even move."

"Ted McKinnon may not want the police tramping through the house," the elder Crissman decided. "Suppose we have a look at this, and see what it amounts to before we call them?"

Expectantly he turned to his detective guest, and Jim Hanley resigned himself to plain "Murder" in earnest. With the other four men of the party he drove to the McKinnon place and left the car in the dead leaf littered driveway. Quietly, they approached the rear of the building and tried the door. It opened and they stepped into the kitchen—to freeze in their tracks, their skins prickling.

"Eat—yuh hear me?" Happy Harry's high-pitched voice came from the floor above. "How many times I gotta tell yuh, yuh gotta eat? How do yuh expect to grow up this way?" He wheedled, like a mother with a stubborn child. "Maybe yuh're cold, huh? Maybe I better tuck you in better."

Despite himself, Hanley felt an eerie chill trickle down his spine as he softly lead the way upstairs. In the upper hallway, they gathered, tiptoed toward a rear door that stood open —and stopped there, rooted in their steps, their mouths gaping.

For a moment they could not fully glimpse the occupant of the bed that half-filled the little room. Happy Harry, sitting on a chair beside it, leaned forward, and partly blocked their vision, but he straightened and shook his head discouragedly—and they stared into the hollow eyes of a shrunken-faced corpse! A ghastly skeleton face that was a little more than darkly discolored skin drawn tight over bones—with a trickle of pulpy cereal drooling sickeningly from between the pried open jaws!

The body lay stretched out in the bed, head and shoulders propped up on a folded pillow. A blanket had been drawn close beneath the chin, but it had fallen away sufficiently to give a glimpse of a sere, a mummy-like neck and bony shoulders. The horribly desiccated corpse of a woman!

"The murdering fool—he killed her and dragged her body up here!" A shocked exclamation broke from one of the onlookers— and the tin cup filled with soured cereal dropped from Happy Harry's fingers and clattered to the table on which he was about to set it.

Like a trapped animal, he leaped to his feet and flung around to face them. Wild fright flared in his balding eyes; stark terror that was shot through with panicky fear for that gruesome thing on the bed. He backed in front of it, shielding it with his cringing, trembling body, as if to stop them from taking it away from him.

"I ain't done nothin' to her—I ain't done nothin'!" He babbled. "They brung her here and left her. I been takin' care of her, that's all. I been lookin' after her. But I can't make her eat. Maybe *you* c'n do something with her," he became suddenly hopeful, as Hanley approached the bed. "Maybe *you* c'n get her to eat?"

"Who brought her here, Harry?" Hanley asked quietly.

"The fellers in the car," Harry's perpetual grin came back as his fear ebbed. "I seen 'em from Mart Corbett's orchard. I seen 'em in the drive, and when I come up close, I seen 'em carry her in. I come up here after they was gone, and she was there in bed. They never came back, so I've been lookin' after her."

"How long ago was that, Harry?" Hanley pressed gently.

"Le'ssee—le'ssee," the half-wit mumbled. "Two weeks—two weeks yesterday— 'cause I go to Corbett's on Sat'days."

Two weeks—but the corpse looked as if it had been lying there for months! For years! In two weeks, a dead body ought to have been well on the way to dissolution, even in that cold room; but here there was no sign of decomposition, scarcely any odor of putrefaction when Hanley drew back the blanket and stared at the wasted skeleton between the sheets.

The body was nothing but skin and bones, the desiccated flesh shriveled away to mummy-nothingness. Hanley bent closer to examine the throat, and his eyes narrowed gingerly. He picked up one of the bony arms to scrutinize the wrist; then the other. In a dozen places there were discolorations much darker than the deep parchment hue of the rest of the skin. Discolorations that surrounded tiny scores that appeared in sets of four—as if sharp teeth had sunk deep into the flesh.…

"This body has not decayed because there is almost nothing left to rot," he told the others as he turned to face their questioning eyes. "It has been drained of blood. Not all at once, as if an embalmer had started to work on it. Over a period of time—how long God only knows!" He pointed to those sets of scores, one after the other. "Some of these are older than others; some have almost disappeared—"

"You mean—" Crissman's tongue wet his dry lips—"do you mean that this woman—"

"This girl," Hanley corrected. "Look at her nails." He lifted a gaunt hand and displayed the coral tinted ovals. "The hair—the teeth. A young girl, scarcely more than 20, I should say."

"You mean that this girl was kept a helpless prisoner, while her blood was drained out of her—while something fed upon her" Crissman's voice was a horse whisper. "You mean that Happy Harry—"

That was not what Jim Hanley meant, but it was the conclusion to which the police jumped immediately. They scoffed at the notion that there might be any truth to Happy Harry's wild story. Who would break into a strange house and put an unknown corpse to bed there? The half-wit had lured the girl to the house or had kidnapped her and dragged her there. He had murdered her slowly and horribly; and then tried to feed her in hope of reviving her and prolonging the hellish nightmare. That was the charge on which they jailed him.

One of the guests at the Crissman house party was a newspaper man. He seized eagerly upon the sensational front page story that was dropped into his lap and made the most of it. By the time Jim Hanley returned to the city the following afternoon the New York papers were full of Westchester's ghastly vampire murder. It shared headlines with another sensational raid of the Wolf Pack. They had made a quarter-million dollar haul while robbing one of the city's largest banks—and had left a trail of savagely torn and mangled bodies in their wake.

Hanley's part in the discovery of the Yorktown Heights corpse had not been overlooked. No identification of the wasted corpse had been possible; nor had the police uncovered any further leads to the murderer. They were making no real efforts, Hanley knew; they were satisfied that Happy Harry was guilty—and yet he could not convince himself that the grinning half-wit was a blood lusting killer....

He had been in his office no more than an hour when the telephone snapped him out of his puzzled meditation. The caller introduced himself as Leland Garrison, a broker, who lived near Riverside Drive.

"I read about your experience in Yorktown Heights, Mr. Hanley; that is why I am calling you," his voice came nervously over the wire. "That corpse—I believe I can furnish you with evidence that will help you discover the killers. If you will come here—"

"Evidence of that sort should be turned over to the Westchester authorities," Hanley cut in impatiently. "My connection with the discovery of the corpse was accidental. I am not interested in the case."

"Yes—yes, I know," the nervousness heightened to frantic anxiety. "It isn't just that, Mr. Hanley. I need you myself. I am convinced that I am in great danger—in deadly peril. I want to retain you. I want you to help me before it is too late. My—" His words, clipped off in midsentence, were followed by momentary silence. "I can't talk now," they came again; tense, hurried, hushed words. "*Please* come and see me—in about an hour. I will be looking for you then, and I will pay anything you ask—only *please don't fail me!*"

Thoughtfully Hanley lowered the receiver while that hoarse plea still jangled in his ear. Someone evidently had come into the house, or had approached the telephone in the midst of the conversation; someone Garrison feared, or distrusted. But what could the man know about that blood-drained corpse in Yorktown Heights?

It would take a little more than twenty minutes to taxi to Garrison's home. The intervening time Henry utilized to investigate his prospective client. Leland Garrison, he learned, was about sixty years old; a wealthy stockbroker, who was in semi-retirement. Much of his business was transacted from his house. He was a widower; had a son, Harvey, who was associated with him in the business, and lived with him. Quiet, eminently respectable people; no scandal or adverse publicity had ever attached to them.

Hardly the sort of man who would nervously imagine himself in danger after reading a sensational newspaper account, Hanley mused as he taxied uptown; hardly the sort of man one would expect to be suspicious of his intimates—

Jim Hanley's eyes swept down the street as the cab turned into Garrison's block, picked out the broker's residence—and sensed in a flash that he was already too late. An automobile stood in front of the building—a coupe with a physician's license number, and a Red Cross attached to the plate!

S wiftly he sped across the sidewalk and up the half dozen steps to the front doors. The outer door opened when he turned the knob, and the inner one stood ajar. He waited for no bell to announce him. Across the wide hallway he strode, his eyes probing, his ears keenly alert—to catch the muffled sound of a horrified gasp. From the back room....

Hanley covered the distance noiselessly, loomed in the doorway—and stared in at a tableau that chilled his blood.

The man who must be Leland Garrison lay stretched awkwardly on the floor, while a bald-headed, thin-faced man, with the unmistakable bearing of a doctor, knelt beside him, a hand probing beneath his open shirt. Behind them, a young woman was backed against the wall, her horrified eyes bulging, the back of one fist jammed into her mouth to stifle the hysteria that threatened to overwhelm her.

That much Hanley saw in a glance, and then his eyes were riveted on the ghastly sight that held her transfixed—on Garrison's throat. Or, rather, on what had been his throat. Now the flesh was gone, torn away to leave a huge, gaping hole from which a crimson flood had spilled out over his clothing—torn away as if a ravening beast had ripped and slashed at it with barbarous abandon!

The physician's task was finished. His face was grim and hard-eyed as he rose to his feet, and then he saw Hanley, stared at him curiously, half-hostilely. He lit a cigarette.

"And who are you?" He demanded gruffly. "The police, I suppose—now that it is too late."

"Jim Hanley, private investigator," Hanley told him. "Mr. Garrison telephoned me about an hour ago, and asked to come here. He seemed to think he was in danger."

"If you had come then, you might have prevented this," the physician grumbled, as he started rearranging his open bag. "This happened no more than half an hour ago. I just arrived here in response to Miss Brinley's summons."

"I—I found him like that when I came in," the girl gasped, as she tried to tear her eyes away from the bloody welter. "I—I am Ann Brinley—Mr. Garrison's secretary. I came up from the office with letters for him to sign. I used my key when nobody answered the bell—and there he was on the floor. I—I telephoned Dr. Tenant."

Her face was ashen, her eyes horror haunted. There was no doubt of her terror—and yet Hanley, sensed instantly that she was not telling the truth; not all the truth. Could she be the one who had interrupted Garrison's phone call—and done this? That hardly seemed possible—and yet, the way she looked at the doctor —

"There was nobody else in the house?" Hanley glanced from one to the other. "No servants?"

"No, Mr. Garrison had not been eating at home," the girl answered, and Hanley saw that she had taken a dogged grip of herself. "There is only the housekeeper, and she is off this afternoon."

"And his son—Harvey Garrison?"

This time it was Dr. Tenant who answered.

"His stepson, you mean, he corrected acidly. "There you are, Mr. Detective; that's all you need, isn't it? A stepson; that gives you a perfect suspect to pin this on—while the Wolf Pack murderers, who are terrorizing this entire city, go unmolested! Well, Mr. Harvey was not here either. Miss Brinley tells me he is out of town today on business. So you will have to look elsewhere—"

"That's where you are wrong doctor," Hanley cut him short. "You have lost a patient, and I seem to have lost a possible client. The difference is that you were already engaged; I was not. My connection with the case ended before it even began."

"Just as well, just as well," the old man huffed. "Private detectives and police, they're all alike. Garrison was a fool to trust his life to them. If he had come to me— That's too late now, but it isn't too late for me to see that he is avenged. Detectives! Bah—I don't need a detective to smoke out a bloodthirsty murderer!"

He was still fuming and giving vent to his contempt for police in general and detectives in particular, when Hanley started into the hallway. He had reached the door and opened it when he saw that Ann Brinley was coming after him, walking quickly to catch up with him.

"Mr. Hanley—please," she called softly as he moved out onto the steps. "I—there is something I want to tell you!"

Suddenly her eyes widened, became great pools of dread. She was staring over his shoulder, out into the street; staring as if she were hypnotized—and then she was grasping his hand, stuffing something into it.

"Take this—take—" she gasped; and her voice was drowned by the short crack of a shot—one and then swiftly another as she staggered backward and clutched at the door jamb.

Instinctively Hanley flung himself against the building as he whirled, his hand flashing to his gun. But that split second was sufficient for the killer. Hanley caught a fleeting glimpse of an indistinguishable figure crouched over the wheel of the doctors coupe, and then the car leaped away from the curb and arrowed down the street to merge with traffic at the corner.

Those shots had been close, so close that one of them had nicked the edge of his coat—but they had been even closer for Ann Brinley. When he turned back into the doorway the girl was slumped over the threshold. Blood crimsoned her dress from a wound in her chest, and the second bullet had torn its way through the side of her head.

She was dead, and on the floor beside her lay the crumpled card she had tried to thrust into his hand—a curious card in the shape of a coffin. Up from its head end grinned a Mephisthophelean face beside the red lettered announcement—*Dracula is waiting for you!*

Chapter 2.
Crimson Kiss

Something about that strange card made Hanley instinctively want to hide it. He reached down for it, but before his fingers closed over the evil leering face he knew that Dr. Tenant was beside him, knew that the physician's eyes were fixed upon him. Hanley palmed the card.

Had Tenant seen what he picked up? There was no way of telling. The physician's eyes were inscrutable, his face was grim when he knelt down beside the girl's body and quickly verified her death. His bleak eyes turned on Hanley with a gaze that almost accused him of being responsible for this latest murder.

"Murder on murder," he muttered. "Murder on murder. Where will it end?"

That was what Jim Hanley asked himself as he looked down at the blood stained corpse of the second person who tried to confide in him that afternoon. The Garrison case had ended for him before it even began, but this, he told himself grimly, was another matter. Perhaps Ann Brinley had not actually retained him, but she had paid with her life to put him on the track of her employer's murderer—and now he had a score to settle with the barbarous Wolf Pack. Jim Hanley's face was grim.

Those shots had aroused the neighborhood. Wide-eyed spectators, were beginning to gather in the street, and he could already hear the distant wail of a police siren. Before the radio car arrived he stepped back into the building and drew the crumpled card from his pocket.

It was about four inches long, and two wide, a hand around which advertised the Dracula, a spooky nightclub that had recently become one of the town's most popular bizarre hotspots. Just the card and nothing more; not even a notation to give a hint of why she had given it to him....

Before he had time to wonder about that the police had arrived; the sirening radio car, and three others hot on its heels. Two more murders to be charged up against the rapacious Wolf Pack brought a dozen Homicide men rushing to the house; but when they had finished their investigation, they knew even less about these latest outrages than Hanley—for they had not seen the coffin card that was tucked away in his vest pocket.

Dracula, the vampire…. Hanley thought of the blood drain corpse Happy Harry had been tending…. The papers had promptly dubbed that a "vampire murder"…. But what possible connection could there be between Happy Harry's ghastly patient up there in Yorktown Heights and this Broadway night club? Had the connection been only in poor Ann Brinley's imagination?

Those questions were running through his mind as he turned off Broadway into the side street, where the baleful green light of the Dracula's sign stood out starkly among its neighbors. Housed in an old, gloomy-looking brownstone building, the somber effect had been enhanced by a first-floor front that simulated the entrance to an ancient tomb; a dimly lighted, creepy looking hiatus in that block of gay neon signs and light-splashing windows.

He had almost reached the doorway when his keen eyes spotted a shadowy figure lurking in the half-alleyway that ran between the Dracula's side exit and its next door neighbor. A watcher! And a clumsy one, at that. Heading forward to get a better look at Hanley, the fellow stepped into a beam of reflected light—and Hanley recognized the thin face of Dr. Arthur Tenant!

So the physician *had* glimpsed the Dracula card…. And here he was, outside the nightclub, on the trail of Leland Garrison's murderer!

The interior of the Dracula carried out the same funeral motif as the entrance. It was designed to represent an underground cavern, a huge burial crypt. The imitation stone walls were hung with withered wreaths and grave-urns filled with immortelles. The flickering light from tall, death-watch candles dimmed rather than added to the weird illumination that played on the strange tables that formed a wide crescent around the highly polished black dance-floor—tables that were wooden coffins standing on low gravestones.

The place was fairly well filled when Hanley entered, but he was able to get a table near the front at one end of the crescent; a location from which he could study the white-faced guests, and the cassock-clad waiters who served them. That unhealthy pallor was a trick of the lighting, he decided; a trick that made the patrons ghost-faced and staring-eyed.

Half a dozen of those pallid faces seemed to be watching him, seemed to be staring at him hungrily, but he recognized none of them. He recognized nobody in the place, so that did not seem to be the reason Ann Brinley had wanted him to come there. But if not that—

At that moment the overhead lights blinked out, and the only illumination came from the candles—until a weird, green radiance enveloped the dance-floor and the Dracula floor show was under-way. Phil Savold, the club's proprietor, boasted that his girls were the most beautiful on Broadway, and Hanley had to agree with him as he watched the score of dancers glide out upon the polished floor. They were lovely young things, all of them, but that cold green light gave them a horribly unearthly hue. It was as if they were dying on their feet.

Dying and decomposing as they danced in a thin line, trailing costumes that were so like grave cerements!

Hanley saw their faces becoming gaunt and thin; saw all the bones rising as the flesh fell away and pools of greenish putrescence formed in the sunken cheeks, in the hollowed eye caverns; saw all the limbs shrink and fade away—saw lovely girlish faces transform into horrible grinning death's-heads that brought gasps and sub-dued shrieks from the watchers.

Dancing corpses rotting away to skeletons!

Lights, of course, he told himself; lights that operated on the X-ray principle—but the effect was horribly realistic. So realistic that the atmosphere of the place became suddenly changed, became rank with the feel of death, with the foul breath of unthinkable evil.

Not only that opening dance. One macabre number followed the other. Ghosts materialized from nowhere, unholy revenants stalked out of the darkness, dull-eyed zombies plodded through their robot ritual. The dismal spell of the grave spread out over them, encompassed them—and those pleasure-jaded fools reveled in it. They applauded and called for more—until part of the lids of the coffins in front of them opened and they stared into the still faces of realistic corpses!

Waxen figures, Hanley solved that one, but he admitted that the verisimilitude was remarkable. The pretty face that looked up at him from the coffin at which he sat was so real that he could almost feel the touch of her chill flesh....

That was the moment when Dracula made his stealthy way out onto the ebon floor. The Dracula of the card Hanley still had in his pocket. A man clothed entirely in black and wearing a tight fitting silk mask from which the card reproduction had been made. He was alone in the pool of green light, and the hushed room was so still it seemed he was alone there as well, except for the coffins.

His body fairly trembled with eagerness as he hurried to one in the center of the crescent and lifted the lid clear. For a moment he bent over the edge and when he came erect a white-clad figure lay in his arms; a limp figure so realistic that it seemed impossible she could be a wax dummy. Back to the center of the floor he carried her, and then the temptation seemed to become too great. Suddenly he bent over her, his open mouth avidly seeking her throat.

Dracula, the vampire, satisfying his unholy appetite!

J im Hanley watched that grizzly performance as attentively as any of those around him. A cold trickle ran slowly down his spine as the eeriness of it gripped him—but suddenly his hands balled into white-knuckled fist, his jaws clenched tightly.

That limp figure in Dracula's arms was no dummy, no wax doll! He had seen the slim legs move; had seen them twitch and writhe in pain! The girl's mouth was open as if to gasp in agony; her eyelids fluttered—and a thin trickle of blood ran down her white neck as the crimson lips of the masked face relinquished their ghastly kiss, and momentarily hovered over her.

That girl was alive and helpless in the clutch of a bloodsucking monster! In full view of those fascinated, stupidly staring eyes she was being held by a human vampire! This was why Ann Brinley had wanted him to come to this diabolical hell-hole; this was the message death had silenced before she could utter it!

Dracula's performance came to an abrupt end as the low music resumed and the chorus danced out onto the floor. They closed in around him, forced him to drop the body of his victim and shooed him off into the wings—where an unscheduled welcome awaited him.

While every eye was fixed on the culmination of that ghastly spectacle, Jim Hanley had risen and made his way unnoticed to the back-stage entrance, only a few yards from where he was sitting. The outpouring of dancers served his purpose excellently. They momentarily screened him from view and enabled him to step from the shadows, and through the doorway without being no-ticed.

Back-stage was at that instant deserted. The full company was out on the floor—and now the masked Dracula was starting back toward the exit. Hanley glanced around him, spied a strand of scenery that offered concealment and stepped behind it.

Once the ebon-clad figure was out of view of the audience his movements became swift and furtive. He glanced around him ner-vously, darted toward a door at the rear; but before he reached it Hanley stepped out in his path and jammed an automatic into his middle.

The eyes behind the mask widened in wild alarm; the crimson lips parted. Yes, they *were* crimson—wet blood that had dribbled down onto the fellow's chin, down onto his ink black garment.

Horror prickled Jim Hanley's scalp as he recognized the gleam-ing red stains. Before the fellow could move, his hand darted out and gripped the silk mask at one ear, fastened in it and tore it away —to bare a terrified face he recognized instantly. Ashen hued and thin, but the face of Harvey Garrison, as he had seen it in the pho-tographs Dr. Tenant had produced for the police that afternoon!

Harvey Garrison—his stepfather's murderer! Harvey Garri-son—a member of the bloodthirsty Wolf Pack!

Ann Brinley must have arrived at the house in time to inter-rupt the horrible ghoul before his noxious task was completed. She must have glimpsed him as he escaped. That was the reason for her terror, the reason why she was murdered before she could reveal what she had seen. Even as the pieces fell into place, Hanley's hand fastened on Garrison's shoulder and whirled him around to jab the gun into his ribs.

"All right, Garrison, we're going out of here—quick, if you want to reach the street alive," he clipped.

"I—I—you can't —" the trembling, captive blubbered, but the automatic prodded him forward, toward a door with an exit sign above it. "Listen—please. You—you have to listen!" His babble rose hysterically as his sweat beaded face turned back over his shoulder. "You —"

At that moment the chorus came dancing off the stage. Hanley glimpsed them out of the corner of his eye, prodded his captive harder—and then it happened. One of the girls suddenly whirled out of nowhere and crashed into him. She threw out her arms to break her fall, clutched at him, and they went down together. Instantly he scrambled back to his feet, but that split second of freedom had been sufficient for Harvey Garrison to reach the exit and dart through it.

Hanley raced after him, flung through the doorway into the dark alley—just in time to see his man leap into a cab that was already starting away from the curb. Hanley's eyes were on the taxi as he reached the street, holding it as it sped toward the corner. Another glided up to the curb; the driver leaned back to open the door, and Hanley jumped in.

"That cab ahead—follow —" he began; and the words died on his lips as a gun barrel rammed into his side and another pressed hard and cold against his neck.

"Sit down, Bud. Sit down and take it easy. He knows where he's going," a brittle voice commanded, and he sank back between two wary-eyed gunmen who frisked him expertly.

Trapped neatly, Hanley admitted glumly. They had been all ready for him, and he had walked into their arms. Two pallid-faced thugs who had the indelible stamp of killers. They watched him like hawks as the taxi approached Fifth Avenue, and he caught the telltale whitening of their knuckles as they gripped their guns more firmly, the betraying glint in their eyes. Once they were across the avenue, once they were in the quiet of the deserted block beyond, they would let him have it....

But that moment never came. The traffic light was just changing as the cab reached the corner. The driver stepped on the gas to get through. Nervously, one of the thugs leaned forward to see whether they would make it—and in that moment Hanley struck. With a cat-like leap, he hurled himself forward against the front of the compartment, while his right fist swept up and drove into the off-guard thug's face. In the same whirlwind motion, he whipped around and warded off the automatic that was clubbing down at his head, grasped the killer's wrist and twisted it with every ounce of strength he could muster—twisted it until the fellow's tortured finger constricted on the trigger, and the gun roared.

The bullet whistled by Hanley's head—and buried itself in the thug, who was about to pounce down on his shoulders. His gasp and moan of pain were echoed by his partner's vicious curses—and then that worthy pitched forward, half-way onto the driver's seat, to collide with the man at the wheel and send the car skittering crazily to one side of the street. Brakes squealed as the driver struggled for control, the cab skidded, precariously, and before it came to a stop the captive leaped clear, and was racing toward Fifth Avenue.

Hanley saved his neck, but with that cab went his hope of contacting Harvey Garrison and his Wolf Pack mates, he dejectedly admitted. Young Garrison had disappeared. How completely, he realized the next day when he failed to contact the young broker at his home or his office, failed to find a trace of him in any of his usual haunts.

Every lead had failed when Hanley turned to Dr. Tenant. How cooperative the sleuthing physician would be was a question, but at least there was a chance that he might know Garrison's whereabouts.

But when he called at Tenant's residence, a stoney-faced English doorman greeted him with raised eyebrows.

"The doctor has no office hours today, sir," he informed. "On Tuesday afternoons he holds surgery."

"Surgery?" Hanley looked blank. "At what hospital is that?"

"It is not held in a hospital, sir," the doorman corrected. "The surgery is Dr. Tenant's charity." And he gave an address far down on the lower East Side.

"Surgery" was the English term for a dispensary, for office hours at a nominal fee, or on a charity basis, Hanley recalled as he taxied downtown. Evidently Tenant maintained a separate office in the slums for this purpose, instead of contributing his charity services to a hospital.

The office, he found, was on the first floor of a partially remodeled tenement in the middle of a squalid, poverty stricken block that teamed with humanity. The entrance was somewhat better than that of the neighboring buildings, but the moment he stepped into the dimly lit hallway the mingled odors of stale cooking and age old mustiness assailed him.

With relief he stepped into the doctor's white-painted reception room, but instantly he sensed that there was something wrong. The middle-aged nurse who sat at a desk towards the rear of the room was fighting desperately to maintain her self control. Her face was a mask, but she could not keep the terror out of her eyes, could not stop the trembling of her fingers. She looked like a woman who was steeling herself for a thunderous explosion that would go off at any moment. When she tried to speak, her lips made only dry, unintelligible sounds, but her eyes turned toward the door to the rear of her desk—a closed door that was not quite able to muffle the voices that came from behind it.

"Stop that shaking, Doc," a heavy voice warned. "Take it easy. We don't want no slips—and neither do you, if you know what's healthy for you. Watch yourself."

That Voice.... Hanley recognize it. The voice of one of the thugs who had tried to kidnap him last night!

Automatic in hand, he cat footed to the door and listened. Now there was another voice, groaning in pain. The doctor's echoed it, trembling, pleading, begging for his life. They must have him at gunpoint, forcing him to dress a wound—and then—

Hanley did not wait for that. His hand gripped the door knob, turned it softly, thrust the door open—and he confronted his captors of the night before. One was stripped to the waist, having a bullet wound dressed. Another held a gun on Dr. Tenant, while the erstwhile driver fingered another gun for good measure.

They gaped at the doorway in astonishment, too stunned to go into action, but before Hanley could take a step toward them there was a slight noise at his back, and something crashed down on his head as the nurse screamed shrilly.

Of course, he berated herself bitterly, there must've been another thug posted in the outer room to keep the nurse covered!

That blow sent him to his knees, but he did not drop his gun. He triggered it twice as he staggered up, almost blinded with pain, and then it was knocked out of his hand. With a rush, the thugs closed in, snarling savage curses, but he managed to grasp one of their guns. By a superhuman effort, he tore it from the fellow's hand, used it as a club to hammer at their heads.

But that struggle could not last; it was too uneven. They overwhelmed him. He went down again. Dimly he heard what sounded like running footsteps, like fists pounding on the door. Another shot roared and his assailants seemed to flee—but not before another savage blow over his throbbing head plunged him deep into billowing darkness....

A sharp sting that spread out as it bored deep into the flesh brought him back to consciousness, to find himself lying on the floor with Dr. Tenant bending over him, a hypodermic syringe in hand.

"They were frightened off—but they may return," the physician quavered. "I did not dare let you remain helpless. I administered a restorative to bring you around."

He stepped back, and dabbed a wet compress against the side of his bald head, brought it down, stained with blood. All the hostility, all the acid gruffness, had gone out of him.

"I think, perhaps the detective business is a little out of my line, Mr. Hanley—if this is a sample of it," he admitted ruefully.

And in that moment, Jim Hanley wondered whether it was not out of his line as well. Three times he had let members of the Wolf Pack slip through his fingers—and it was only a miracle that he was not by now a torn in mutilated corpse.

Chapter 3.
Choice of a Lifetime

Connie Stewart's fortunes had just about hit bottom the afternoon she trudged back to the rooming house that would cease to be her home the moment her suspicious, landlady, lost patience and locked her out. It was more than ten weeks since her show had folded up—after a three-week run; and since then, she had made the rounds of agencies and producers in vain. She would have gone back home to Joplin, Missouri, had there been any home or family to go to; but there wasn't.

She was finished, washed up, that afternoon, when she found Gwen Coman waiting for her.

Gwen was a girl with whom she had danced in the "Let There Be Love" company. They had been very friendly during the rehearsal and the show's short-lived existence, but after that they had seen nothing of each other—until Gwen suddenly appeared with another girl, somewhat older than herself. Gwen rose to her feet.

"This is Mona Kenyon—I'm getting married. He's a millionaire, Connie—Dick Van Alst, a boy with scads of do-re-mi!" The pretty redhead accomplished her introduction and made her triumphant announcement all in one breath. "I'm stepping off tomorrow—that's why we're here—I want to toss my bridal bouquet in your lap!" she battled on. "Not really that, you know—I won't really have a bouquet—no time for that—we're slipping off for a quiet ceremony and then on our way!"

It was Mona Kenyon, who took charge of the conversation and made it intelligible when they were seated in Connie's room.

"Gwen has been living with me; we both work at Phil Savold's Dracula," she explain. "That's where she met her diamond-studded wonder. Now that she's walking out on me I'm looking around for someone to share my apartment. Last night I saw your photo while she was packing her stuff, and she told me about you. I thought you might be interested, Connie—"

She left the invitation unfinished as her eyes inventoried the cheaply furnished room.

"But I am not working," Connie confessed. "I haven't been since they closed up 'Let There Be—'"

"That's what I thought," Gwen swept aside her objection. "Don't worry about that. Mona's a great little fixer. She got me into the Dracula; she'll fix it for you. Leave it to her. Once you're working for Phil Savold, you're as good as married to a million. We've got a wedding bell batting average at the Dracula that puts it all over any other place in town. It's a regular happy hunting grounds for the banknote boys!"

"With your looks, and your figure," Mona Kenyon nodded, as her gaze traveled appreciatively over Connie's slim, full-breasted form, "I think I may be able to work it. I know pretty well what Savold likes."

And she did.

It all seemed unbelievable to Connie Stewart, all part of a fantastic dream, from which she would certainly be distressingly awakened. First, the switch to Mona Kenyon's sumptuously furnished apartment, and then, two days later, an introduction to Phil Savold —and she was hired, engaged for the floor show that had become every New York chorine's goal.

The chance of a lifetime had come her way, she congratulated herself as she left the office of the little man who had become a virtual Broadway Cupid, but her elation could not quite smother the strange twinge of apprehension that had coursed through her as she underwent Savold's inspection. There was something about the short, bullet headed man, something about his thick-lipped, flat-nosed face, his dark, cynical eyes that made her shudder.

There was something about his probing eyes that was different—and terrifying.

I mpatiently, she shrugged off such thoughts, but when she stepped into the Dracula with Mona for her first rehearsal her scalp prickled, and the uneasiness crept back into her brain. No nightclub was ever cheery looking or inviting in the morning, with chairs piled on tables, with the stale odors of the last night's festivities still heavy on the air—but the Dracula was more distasteful than any she had ever seen. The atmosphere was rank, almost choking.

The chairs piled carelessly on those coffins…. The faded flowers on the walls looking even more forlorn in the thin daylight that filtered into the place…. The extinguished candles…. All combined to create an air of desolation, of haunting evil, it made her shiver with revulsion.

The Club Dracula, the morning after, was like a slatternly old beldame waking up from a drunken orgy.

"Gets under your skin, doesn't it?" Mona Kenyon read her thoughts. "That's what gets the customers—the atmosphere. Most of the girls feel a little squeamish at first, but you'll get used to it."

Perhaps, Connie told herself, but the more she saw of the Dracula's routine, the more it depressed her. These were not ordinary dances, not merely extra-bizarre numbers, instinct told her. There was something more behind them—but what? Something unclean, unwholesome; something that made her long to get out of the place and fill her lungs with cold, purifying fresh air.

She wished now that she had more opportunity to ask Gwen Coman about the club, but Gwen had been so wrapped up with her wedding preparations she had no time and thought for nothing else. And Mona? She did not like to question Mona too closely for fear of seeming critical and unappreciative; Mona seemed to take the atmosphere of the Dracula so much for granted.

Even when she shrank from the necessity of having a mask of her face made for her wax double that was to go into one of the coffins, Mona only laughed at her.

"It—it's like watching yourself being buried alive!" She whispered, as the dummy-maker finished his task and laid out his newest "corpse." "It looks so real—I almost feel that it is me!"

"Sure," Mona chuckled, "that's what we want the customers to think. They get a kick out of it, seeing the girls on the floor and then finding them in the coffin tables. Phil Savold is a genius that way—he sure knows what they want."

Phil Savold not only knew what his customers wanted; he knew what *he* wanted as well, Connie discovered before her first week had ended. It was after the second floor show one night that he cornered her backstage. She had changed her costume and was on her way to the floor to take her place at a table with one of the customers, when he stepped into her path and blocked her way.

"You're doing fine, babe," he complimented. "I've been watching you plenty. I like your style. I—"

Something about his smile, about the gleam in his cloudy eyes, warned her, but she was not prepared for the speed with which he suddenly swept her into his arms. Before she could more than gasp, he held her fast, in a grip she could not break, while his lips found hers and possessed them hungrily, savagely.

"You've got everything, babe," he panted. "You and me—we can go places together. We can show this town."

Kiss after kiss he rained upon her, until she was struggling for breath, fighting him off, desperately. Free at last, she staggered back, her arms desperately raised to ward him off, her eyes blazing with scorn that he could not fail to read. His eyes narrowed, and his thick lips pressed together as he stared at her, his brain trying to comprehend this thing that had happened to him.

"So I'm not good enough for you, eh?" He snarled. "I'm not pretty enough, I suppose—or maybe you have all your cap set for one of those gold-plated playboys outside? You want to cop one of the gold rings, eh? You poor fool, I'm giving you a chance at something real. I'm giving you a chance at more real cash than you'll ever see. A chance to get out of this town and see something of the world. Don't be a sap."

This time Connie was ready for him when he lunged forward.

"No—no—please!" She pleaded as she tried to hold him off, and at that moment Mona Kenyon stepped out of the shadowy passageway that led to the dressing rooms.

For an instant Connie glimpsed her roommate's wide eyes fixed upon them. Round eyes that blazed with fury. And then Phil Savold was backing away, grinning imperturbably.

"OK, Connie, I'll fix things up for you," he promised. "I'll see that you're taken care of properly, don't worry about that—just leave it to old Phil."

With that he was gone, but his mocking threat rang in Connie's ears, and his gleaming eyes struck terror deep into her heart. His eyes had smiled, but out of their murky depths had blazed a flame of unholy vindictiveness. For an instant she had gazed upon demoniacal wickedness starkly unmasked....

"That is something else I should've told you about," Mona Kenyon said evenly. "Don't take Phil too seriously; he tries out his line on all the new girls."

But was that all? Fervently Connie wished that she could believe it, but she could not drive out of her memory what she had seen. It hung over her, oppressed her with a dread foreboding, with a persistent premonition that she was in the presence of something unthinkably infamous. A nebulous premonition that suddenly took appalling shape!

The Dracula number which ended the fourth show never failed to fill Connie with revulsion, but beyond that she had paid it no particular attention. It sent a shiver down her spine to watch the masked performer lift one of the wax dummies from its coffin and go through his horrible ritual, and she dreaded the night when she might have to watch him clutching the effigy which was so like herself. It would almost be like having him take her actual self.

That unpleasant thought was in her mind when she went back to get her purse from the dressing room sometime after the last floor show of the night. It was Carol Leslie whose effigy had been used in the Dracula number that night, and Carol was still in the dressing room changing her clothes, long after all the others had left.

Connie glanced at her in surprise—and was quickly filled with concern. The girl was deathly pale, seemed to sway drunkenly as she fastened her evening dress. Connie hurried forward to help her, but Carol looked at her with lackluster eyes that were devoid of recognition. Glassy eyes. Connie's first thought was that she had been drinking, had been nursing a bottle back there in the dressing room. But there was no odor of alcohol about her—no odor—

And what was that red blotch on her throat?

An angry red blotch that was nearly twice the size of a silver dollar. Connie stared at it with incredulous, horrified eyes. A reddish blotch just where Dracula's blood hungry mouth had fastened on the throat of her effigy... And there, distinguishable in the midst of the discoloration, were four tiny scars—four wounds that might have been made by sharp, slashing teeth!

Wounds that might have been made by a blood-lusting vampire as he sucked the crimson life-fluid from her veins!

Paralyzing horror gripped Connie Stewart as she stared at those tiny marks. She tried to speak, but her tongue was dry; no sound came from her lips. And then there was a rap on the door; Phil Savold opened it.

"What's keeping you, Carol?" He demanded. "Young Gallagher's hollering for you. Had all I could do to stop him from coming back here after you. Come on—let's go."

Without a word Carol went with him; went out to the table, where her wealthy fiancé was impatiently waiting for her. Ten minutes later, when Connie danced past them, the girl seemed to be completely recovered—all except that angry, red splotch, which even the powder she had daubed over it could not conceal....

Chapter 4.
In Love With—What?

Sleep had no power to drive the haunting horror from Connie Stewart's mind that night. Angry red splotches gaped at her out of the darkness like blind, unseeing eyes. Hungry, sharp toothed mouths pursued her, hovered over her throat tantalizingly. Time after time she woke to find her brow wet with perspiration—just as the evil face of a Dracula who looked strangely like Phil Savold faded into nothingness.

It was broad daylight the last time she barely escaped from that slavering mouthed fiend—and when she was able to throw off the brain paralyzing fright that gripped her she realized that the rasp of the apartment buzzer had awakened her. Mona had been awakened too. Connie heard her stirring in her room, heard her crossing the foyer.

Two tall, broad shouldered, man, stood in the doorway when she had slipped on a négligée and peered over Mona's shoulder. Two detectives! They were talking about Gwen Coman—about Gwen Coman's *body*!

"We were able to make a partial identification through a dentist who recognized his work in an upper bridge in the mouth," one of them was saying. "That's why we're here. We want you to come down to the morgue and confirm it."

A *partial* identification by her teeth? But surely the dentist ought to have remembered Gwen's face; nobody who knew that impish redhead would have forgotten her so completely that he could not recognize her. Unless her face… Horror swept over Connie in a numbing wave; horror that seemed to drain the strength from her limbs.

"But—but Gwen isn't here in New York," she managed to gasp. She's on her honeymoon—she's in California with her husband—"

The detective shrugged.

"Maybe so; maybe this dentist is all wrong," he admitted; but she saw that he did not believe what he was saying. She saw that he knew the dentist was right. "Quickest way to settle that is to come Down and see for yourself. We'll wait until you're ready."

Connie's fingers were numb as she hurried into her clothes. Her eyes avoided Mona's fearful of reading in her friend's glance confirmation of the horrible thoughts that were crowding her brain. It seemed an age before they finished dressing, before the detectives' car had sped them downtown and they walked into the chill desolation of the "icebox" room, to a table, where a sheet covered figure lay ready for them.

But *that* could not be Gwen! She had weighed all of a hundred and twenty pounds—and there was *almost nothing* under that sheet!

Connie felt her eyes widening, felt her eyeballs swelling, as she watched the attendant grasp the sheet—to expose a ghastly horror that sent her brain staggering. She reeled back, and would have fallen if one of the detectives had not grasped her in time. He held her up, held her so that she could stare down at the shrunken mummy that had been Gwen!

For a moment her stunned brain would not believe what she saw. That grizzly, grinning corpse, couldn't be Gwen! Surely it was some old woman, shrunken and withered, the crinkly skin discolored with age... But that was Gwen's glorious red hair; yes, and it was her nose, her squared jaw and chin; even the little mole just below her ear. Her chin and—

Suddenly Connie strained forward, her popping eyes riveted on the skinny throat—on a block of discoloration that was darker than the surrounding area. A blotch in which she could distinguish four little scars like the marks of sharp teeth! The dread trademark of Dracula, the vampire!

C onnie knew that she ought to have fainted at that moment, but she seemed to be beyond even that. Over her spread a pall of horror that deadened her senses, that numbed her brain and left her little better than the still figures that filled that store room of death.

Gwen Coman, who had gone off so joyously with her millionaire husband, to end up in little more than a week a desiccated, bloodless corpse on a cold morgue slab!

Her husband—where was he? Connie heard herself asking the question in a voice she hardly recognized as her own.

"We don't know anything about that, miss," one of the detectives told her. "She was found like that, in the back of a sedan that crashed into a telephone pole up on Third Avenue and Ninetieth Street the night before last. The driver got away without being seen. A stolen car."

The police knew nothing about Richard Van Alst, and neither did the girls at the Dracula. Connie questioned them that night, but nobody knew any more about Gwen's husband than that he had been a customer who spent plenty of money. Nobody had heard from her after she had started on her honeymoon.

"How about these other girls who married millionaires—have any of them ever come back here to see you?" Connie's lips framed the question that had been bedeviling her all afternoon. "Have you heard from any of them since they left?"

She knew the answer even before it came. They had not. The girls had gone off with their new husbands—and that was the last the Dracula ever saw, or heard of them. They had gone off—where?

Horror maggots scrolled through Connie's aching brain as she faced the answer to that question. Those bridegrooms—what were they? *Were they human?* Or were they vampires—horrible creatures like that Dracula who strode out onto the dance floor for his revolting performance every night. And what was he? A flesh and blood performer like the rest of them—*or something else?*

Phil Savold made a great mystery of the identity of his grisly star. He was listed on the program as a question mark, and even the rest of the troupe were never permitted to see him unmasked. They knew no more about him than the guests.

A man or a vampire? The audience gasped each night, when the black-garbed figure passed in front of a mirror and cast no reflection in it; but that was a trick, an invisible Polaroid curtain that whipped down over the glass just before he reached it. Connie knew that, but now she asked herself whether the trick was what it seemed—*or to hide the fact that the glass would have been empty when he passed it!*

Perspiration bathed her limbs as she cowered away from that terrifying possibility. Such thoughts were the road to madness, she told herself—were madness itself. There was no such thing as a vampire. That blotch on Carol Leslie's neck had been the result of an accident—a bruise or a burn. Gwen Coman had been murdered; murdered fiendishly, but murdered by a depraved human being. And those teeth marked blotches—

They were accidents, weren't they? Bruises or burns, perhaps? And the blood that had been drained out of her veins—?

Connie clamped her palms to her throbbing temples and tried desperately to flee from those mocking, tantalizing answers. She fled from the dressing room, but in the doorway Phil Savold confronted her, his face wreathed in a smug smile.

"I haven't forgotten my promise, babe," he beamed upon her. "I have a man for you—one of the best catches we ever had in the place. Armand Ladue—from New Orleans. I've got it straight that his family owns half of Louisiana. I'm giving you first chance at him."

He had not forgotten his promise… Connie caught the subtle double entendre tone of his words, the steely glint in the depths of his eyes, and her scalp tightened as she went out with him to meet —what? To meet a tall, well-set-up man with crisp, black hair and pleasant gray eyes. A man whose skin was well tanned, or naturally olive—in striking contrast to the pallid faces of a most of the Dracula's habitues.

Armand Ladue bowed and held a chair for her, and instinctively she knew that she would like him—even though the knowledge sent a trickle of chilling terror down her spine. She must keep up her guard against him, she warned herself; she must fight against his attraction for her as she had never fought anything in her life—but before she had been with him the first hour, she knew that she not only liked, but *trusted* him!

The man broke down her barriers without seeming to make an effort of doing so. It was not his wealth; she thrust that out of her mind. It was himself, the sound of his voice, the flash of his eyes, the personal magnetism that emanated from him. They encompassed her, trapped her—and in the distant shadows she caught a glimpse of Phil Savold watching them and grinning with approval….

Three nights Armand Ladue was out there waiting for her when she appeared after the first floor show—and on the third night she could no longer deceive herself. He had won, she admit-

ted bitterly. He was the man she had always dreamed of meeting—
if he was a man! She was in love with him; in love, with her ideal—
or with a supernatural creature that had to cunning power to counter-
feit all she esteemed in a man!

His understanding eyes seemed to read her terror, seemed to
invite her to confide in him. The flood of words that would un-
leash the full torrent of her freight rushed to her lips, but before she
could utter them it was time to go backstage for the last show of
the night.

As soon as the performance was finished she would tell him,
she made her decision as she started toward the backstage entrance.
As soon as she could get out there to him again, she would unbur-
den her soul to him. As soon as she—

What was making her legs so heavy? They were like leaden
weights; slow, ponderous, things, that moved forward at a snail's
pace. Not only her legs; her arms, too. She could barely lift a hand
to brush aside the curtain as she reached the entrance. And her eyes
—they were so heavy lidded they were closing—closing. She was
stumbling—falling—and everything at which she clutched was
turning into intangible darkness that surged up on every side, to
smother her....

Icy terror sheathed Connie Stewart from head to foot when
she opened her eyes and realized her plight. She was lying on her
back in the dark; lying on her back and unable to move a muscle
even though her hands did not seem to be tied. She was paralyzed,
helpless, could not even cry out although the music of the floor
show was loud in her ears and people who would spring to her aid
must be very close to her.

Very close... That noise above her head, that clinking and
thumping... Now she knew where she was. She was in one of the
coffins! Some unsuspecting revelers were setting down their glasses
on the wooden lid that covered her? She could hear the laughter,
could hear a girl squealing in pretended fright—and the sounds,
came to her as if from another world, a world with which she was
finished.

ow she realized what had happened to her. She was drugged, her body paralyzed, a limp victim lying there and waiting for Dracula! For Dracula and his blood-hungry teeth!

Desperately she tried to move, to scream, to do anything to attract attention, as she heard the show numbers swiftly passing. It was useless. She could only lie there and wait—wait until the music had stopped, until the hushed silence fell over the wide room.

His approach was almost noiseless, but her terror-sharpened ears caught the soft tread of his feet. He was coming! He was right there, above her grasping the coffin lid from which the glasses had been hastily removed. He was lifting it—and now she knew that her eyes were half open. She could see. She could make out his dark figure, could see him bending over her as he lifted her clear of the box.

And then —

God in heaven! She could see his face as he carried her back to the center of the floor—and her last hope crumbled. The face was the face of the mask, but the eyes—the eyes were Armand Ladue's! She knew those gray eyes too well to be mistaken. They were Armand's; and that tanned hand—it was Armand's, too!

Her heart stood still as the leering mask-face bent over her, as his breath beat against her cheek—as his teeth closed on her throat. She steeled herself for the pain as they would sink into her flesh— but she felt only a wet trickle that ran back across her neck and into her hair. Blood! Armand was feasting on her life blood!

That crowning horror was too much. She felt her senses fading, slipping—until suddenly the pain snapped her back to full consciousness. The sharp, stinging pain of his teeth—only, strangely, it was stabbing into her back instead of her throat.

"Get a grip on yourself, Connie!" She heard him whispering sharply close against her ear. "You'll be all right in a few moments—then follow my lead!"

And then, before her dazed brain could comprehend, the wraith chorus came dancing out from the wings to surround them and drive the vampire from his prey....

Chapter 5.
Honeymoon Hell

Jim Hanley retreated before that dancing onslaught, but he had no intention of relinquishing the limp figure that was just beginning to stir in his arms. Back to the wings he made his way slowly, praying desperately that the powerful resuscitative he had injected between her shoulder blades would speedily counteract the effects of the drug that paralyzed her muscles.

Through the wings and into the backstage area he darted before he dared to stand her on her feet, to lean her propped against the wall, while he ran to the property room, where he had tossed Harvey Garrison, bound, and gagged, after knocking him out and stripping the Dracula outfit off him.

There had been no time for planning during the past five minutes. For three days and nights he had been waiting for the break that had come tonight, but it had been sprung so unexpectedly, so diabolically, that he had almost been caught flat-footed. Connie's failure to appear with the chorus in the night's final floor show had been the tip-off that saved him. The moment he spotted her absence he had known that something was wrong—and had gambled that Dracula was behind it.

That gamble had paid double, he congratulated himself grimly. It had knitted young Garrison, the man he was seeking, and had snatched Connie out of the hands of these devils. Now all that remain was to get his prisoner and drag him along as he led the girl to safety....

Gun in hand, he opened the property room door—and leaped back just in time to miss a bludgeon that swung down viciously at his head. He was too late! Garrison had been found. He was on his feet, staggering drunkenly while a pasty faced thug slashed at the rope that bound his wrists; and a second hoodlum had been waiting there for the door to open.

With lightning speed Hanley lunged to counter that blow. The barrel of his weapon smashed down over the thug's skull, but Connie's frightened scream warned him before he leaped in to settle with the other fellow. Something was wrong—and in a moment he saw what it was. These thugs in the property room were not the only ones he had to face; there were three more closing in on Connie.

His gun roared, and one of them dropped in a squirming heap, but the others fell back to cut off the path to the alleyway door—and now his weapon was rendered useless. He could not stand there and trade lead with Connie on his hands. Flight was their only hope. But where?

Shielding her as well as possible with his body, he backed toward the opposite side of the building, his gun blasting a warning shot at the property room door, and then swinging warily to cover a charge from the alleyway entrance. By now pandemonium had broken loose backstage. The chorus had come dancing off—and had fled, shrieking wildly, when his gun barked. That screaming would bring Phil Savold and more of his killers.

Hanley glanced around him, desperately seeking a way of escape, just as one of the girls appeared in a half open doorway, near the property room, hissed and beckoned to them.

"Connie—this way!" She called. "I'll get you out!"

"It's Mona—my roommate," Connie gasped with relief. "She knows this place better than anyone else."

Hanley snatched at the offer. He covered Connie's dash to the doorway with another warning shot, and then sped after her. Quickly Mona closed and locked the door behind them, lead the way across the room and opened the closet. She fumbled inside of it, and one of the walls slid soundlessly upward to afford access to a dimly lighted stairway that led downward.

"This place used to be a speakeasy in Prohibition days," she explained, as she took the lead. "Savold worked here then, and now he uses these trick stairs as a private entrance."

T he stairway went down to a depth of more than two floors. There it terminated in a narrow, cement-walled passageway some twenty feet long. At the end of this was a metal door leading into a little room as bare as the corridor, a room with another of those tight-fitting doors in the wall directly opposite.

That much Jim Hanley saw as Mona switched on the light—and instantly an alarm clambered in his brain. Those doors—metal, airtight! Too late he sprang toward Mona, who had already crossed the room. Before he reached her, the light winked out to plunge them into stygian darkness, and at the same instant he tripped against something almost knee-high; something solid, in a movable, descent, him tumbling headlong.

The agony of his battered shin almost crippled him, but he scrambled to his feet—in time to hear the click of a lock, and then Connie's moan of terror. Carefully, he felt his way to her, over foot-high, room-long barriers that had come up out of the floor. He reached her, got his arm around her, and tried to make his way back to the door by which they had entered; but he knew that was useless.

Already he had caught a whiff of the choking gas that was pouring into the trap. It was clutching at his throat, making his head spin, and his senses reel.

"Armand! Armand!" He heard Connie's faint, far-away voice, calling to him; and the last thing he knew was a great regret that he would never be able to tell her that millionaire Armand Ladue was only a no-account private detective who had had no better sense than to gamble with her affections, and even her life....

Hanley's head felt as big as a balloon when he opened his eyes and blinked around the room that was billowing sickeningly. The gas, he remembered; coming out of it was worse than a hangover. At least it had not been lethal gas. That was something—but when he had time to take a good look around him, he wasn't so sure of that.

He was bound hand and foot, in an underground room, a much larger one than the gas-trap cubbyhole. That was probably the anteroom for this one, he decided; probably lay beyond one of the half dozen doors he could see. This room was very comfortably furnished with rugs, easy chairs, card tables, a radio; a club room, from the look of it.

There were nine occupants besides himself. Connie, looking small and terrified, slumped in a big easy chair, with a slick-haired, pasty-faced killer mounting guard over her. Harvey Garrison, his face ashen-pale, his bloodless lips twitching spasmodically, sat a few feet away, watching her like a hungry dog eyeing a bone he does not dare snatch until permission has been granted. Phil Savold stood leaning back against the table, his arms folded over his chest, a smile that was not good to see pursing in his thick lips. Mona sat near him, puffing on a cigarette, her eyes nervously flickering from one to the other. Even more uneasy was the gray haired, Vandyked old fellow, who clutched a little black, leather bound book—and looked as if he wished he were anywhere but there. Five of the principles, and four of those pallid-skinned, pinch faced thugs; killers with nervously twitching fingers and eyes that were un-healthily bright.

"Come on, snap out of it, Hanley," Savold jeered, when he saw that "Armand Ladue" was conscious. "You're holding up the wedding. Sorry it isn't going to be your wedding, old man, but the lady gave you the go-by when she wised up that her millionaire is only a cheap shamus. You can't get away with that, you know. My girls are very particular; millionaires, or nothing—that's them."

"Oh, no—I didn't—" Connie tried to protest, but her captors fingers sank in her shoulder, yanked her back into the chair, and the half uttered words died on her lips.

"It seemed a shame to disappoint the dominy here," Savold mocked. "He's r'aring to go, so Garrison is going to take your place. Connie might have done better, I suppose, but she can't be choosy now—and Harvey's not such a bad millionaire at that. Now, if you'll sit up and pay attention, Hanley, we'll get started. Okay dominy—shoot."

Hastily the old man stepped to where Garrison had taken his place beside Connie, yanked to her feet by her guard—and that infamous travesty of a marriage began. Connie sobbed heartbrokenly; Hanley damned Phil Savold hopelessly and fought savagely with the rope that held his wrists; Mona watched with narrowed eyes, nervously lighting one cigarette on the butt of another.

A marriage… Marriage to a blood hungry monster… Into Hanley's brain an inkling of what was afoot began to creep—a horrifying inkling of the meaning of this sumptuously furnished room with so many side doors….

The droning words of the marriage service came to an end, and Garrison's arms closed around his trembling bride. Connie's tears had stopped now; had given place to stark terror as she tried to shrink away from him. And in that moment Hanley caught a glimpse of the fellow's eyes. Terrible eyes! The eyes of a wild thing, of a starving animal—and yet, for an instant he was certain he had glimpsed horror equal to the girl's mirrored in them.

"Congratulations, Harvey!" Savold boomed. "Happy honeymoon! We have the bridal chamber already for you. The one down at the end—" he pointed to the farthest door; and Hanley knew that his worst fears were horribly justified.

This concrete catacombs was a hell on earth—a diabolical "honeymoon" hell—a ghastly prison and slaughterhouse! It was here that the girl whose corpse had been found in Yorktown Heights had died. It was here that the Coman girl had been murdered—here that the Dracula "brides" were taken by their supposed "millionaire" husbands! Once they entered the securely hidden rooms they never came out alive; never came out until their shrunken corpses were carried out at night, and driven out of town to be disposed of somewhere miles from New York….

Connie's knees gave way before she had taken half a dozen steps. She crumpled, but Garrison caught her before she fell, swept her up into his arms and bore her off to her doom.

"Please—oh, please!" She sobbed hysterically. "Won't *someone* help me?"

Someone—but that plea was directed straight at Phil Savold. Her imploring eyes met his and held them; beseeching, promising eyes. Even Savold would be preferable to what lay ahead of her. Jim Hanley saw and understood, and his heart bled for her. Savagely he cursed his helplessness and struggled against the rope that held his wrists bound behind his back, ripped and tore at them until his hands were wet with blood.

But that frantic appeal had registered on the nightclub owner. The sardonic smile never left his face, but Hanley saw eagerness leap into his eyes. For a moment he seemed to hesitate, and then, just as Garrison approached the "bridal chamber" door, he started purposely toward them. Started—but was stopped before he covered half the distance; stopped by a blazing-eyed tigress who barred his way.

"No, you don't!" Mona Kenyon flared. "You're staying right out here! I know all about your yen for her, but you're not getting away with it! You're—"

Savold paid no attention to her. He hardly seemed to hear her as he brushed her side—but she was back at him in a flash. Snarling and screaming she hurled herself upon him, she seized his arm and whirled him around to drag him back, slashed out at his face with clawing nails that reached his cheek and drew blood.

"Don't let him get away with it, you fools!" She screamed to the watching thugs. "He's double-crossing you! He's running out on you! He and that doll-face over there—he's going to run off with her and leave you holding the bag. He thinks I've been blind —"

And then Savold turned on her.

Suddenly his right hand darted toward her throat. Not to seize it; to slash and rip at it, to sever the jugular, and loose the crimson fountain of her life-blood!

Mona knew that she was doomed the moment he touched her. Horror filled her eyes, paralyzed her rage-contorted face. She staggered back, tried desperately to protect herself.

"Phil!" His name sobbed from her lips hideously as she crumpled to the floor and rolled over on her back in the crimson lake that spread out beneath her.

That was the moment when Jim Hanley heaved himself out of the chair in which he had been sitting. A hopeless jester? So it seemed. Bound hand and foot, he was utterly helpless to interfere. For an instant he tottered as he struggled to keep his balance; then he toppled headlong, half on top of the dying woman, to roll over on his back—with his bound hands desperately groping for the thing he had seen Savold discard as he turned contemptuously from the woman who had been his sweetheart.

Phil Savold started toward the door where Garrison stood halfway across the threshold—but suddenly he whirled, his hand streaking toward his hip. Too late the import of Mona's screamed warning had registered on his brain. Too late, he realized what it would mean. His gun came up—only to drop from his numbed fingers as a bullet smashed into his arm. A bullet from an automatic in the old clergyman's hand!

A clergyman… Hanley stared at that face, stripped it of hair and Vandyke; stared at the sharp features, the blazing eyes that now transformed it—and recognition that he had half sensed burst fully upon him. And in the same split-second came complete understanding—understanding, and the germ of a desperate plan.…

"Tenant! Dr. Tenant!" He yelled. "You —"

"Hanley, Hanley," the old man chided. "Such shouting of names is indiscreet; you should know that. It might be embarrassing, but not with these gentlemen." He nodded toward the ferret eye thugs. "They are my men—my *trusted* man. Not like you, Savold," he suddenly whipped at the nightclub owner. "I trusted you, too—for a while. I gave you rope enough to hang yourself, and you did exactly what I expected. You thought you were deceiving me completely, but I have been perfectly aware of your treachery. I know that you have tricked young Garrison into looting his own business so that there will be nothing left for me when his stepfather's will is settled. I know that you have been holding out on me right along. I know, too, that your plans for running out on me are all made—I knew that before Mona gave you away just now.

"That's why I insisted on staging this little wedding tonight— so that I could be present myself; not just to make it tougher for Hanley, as you thought. We are all gathered here because I am making a change. You wanted to get out and now you are getting out. I don't need you anymore, but I need the Dracula—to recruit fair brides for my popular 'millionaires.' You are turning the place over to me. I am putting a new manager in charge. Here—" he reached into his pocket for several papers—"are some documents for you to sign. Here is my pen—sign them!"

The gun barrel lifted threateningly, and Phil Savold cowered, abjectly, his ugly face gleaming with perspiration. He picked up the fountain pen with trembling fingers, started scribbling his name without even reading what he was signing.

When Hanley heaved himself out of the chair and toppled to the floor, one of the thugs had quickly stepped to his side and seized him by the collar, to yank him upright and throw him back where he had been—but not before Hanley had seen the unholy gleam that came into the fellow's eyes as he stared at the wide pool of Mona Kenyon's blood. Not until he had seen the fellow's nostrils flare, had seen his tongue edge out hungrily over his dry lips.

This was one of the ravenous Wolf Pack—a human beast who had scented the maddening odor of fresh blood!

Back into his chair Hanley was flung, and the thing he had picked up from the floor stabbed painfully into his flesh. Gingerly he drew it out and fingered it exploringly. It was a glove, as he had thought—a glove equipped with four metal-lined fingers that ended in long, sharp, spike-like claws. A terrible weapon for tearing out a human throat! And a perfect instrument for slicing into soft flesh to start warm blood flowing—and to leave a four-toothed scar!

Carefully Hanley maneuvered the glove between his bound hands until he was able to wriggle one of them into it. Then he started to work on the rope at his wrists, started twisting and squirming, contorting his agonized hands so that those razor-sharp claws could reach the rope. That was a grueling task. The slashing blades bit into his flesh half a dozen times for every time they reached the strands—but the thought of Connie in that room with the blood-mad monster spurred him on heedlessly.

The thought of Connie—and the roar of Dr. Tenant's gun.

Phil Savold had finished his signing. His trembling lips had opened to beg for mercy—and closed when a bullet drove squarely through the center of his head.

"Mr. Savold has gone abroad—for his health, if anyone should inquire about him, Hanley," the cold-blooded killer turned away from the slumped corpse. "You will take charge here for me. These instruments he signed give you a two-year contract as manager and a power-of-attorney. I know that you will use them judiciously."

"Me? Do you think that I am going to do your dirty work?" Hanley laughed, scornfully.

"You are going to be my right-hand man, my active manager," Tenant assured him complacently. "I have been looking for a capable man to replace Savold, and I knew that I had found him when I met you."

"So that's why I was kidnapped at the Dracula, eh?"

"Precisely," Tenant nodded. "You were to be brought to me, but you became a bit too strenuous in your objections. When you obligingly called upon me the next day, we were waiting for you. I gave you your first injection while you were unconscious, and you have been receiving treatments upstairs each night in your drinks. After a few more injections, I am quite sure that you will see the wisdom of cooperating with me."

"After a few more injections, I will be broken and completely under your domination—a drugged slave like Harvey Garrison!" Hanley shouted. "I know exactly what you've been doing to the poor devils who fell into your hands. You've been filling them with a drug that destroys their red blood corpuscles and turns them into anemics. First, you started on your own patients. When their bodies were crying for blood, you brought them to the Dracula and turned them over to Savold. He gave them their first taste of fresh blood when he let them play the Dracula role—and then they were doomed. You made them your abject slaves and forced them to turn over much of their fortunes to you. You made them sell their stocks and bonds—everything they possess—just to satisfy your greed.

"Then you became more ambitious. You decided to go in for crime in a big way—so you opened your charity office in the slums and proceeded to victimize the thieves and hoodlums who came to you for treatment. That's the answer to the Wolf Pack—a gang of blood hungry anemics who are rewarded for the loot they are turning over to you by the horrible portions of human blood you dole out to them!"

"Well reasoned so far," Tenant nodded, sober approval. "But you have overlooked one other point concerning the so-called Wolf Pack which, as my manager, it is best that you understand."

"No, I haven't overlooked it," Hanley roared, as sudden inspiration came to him. "Making anemics of those poor devils isn't all you have done to them. There is no 'so-called' about it—they are a pack of wolves! You have been treating them with serum, or perhaps even transplanting wolf glands into them to whet their appetite for blood. You, a physician they came to for help—*you have turned them into human wolves!*"

By the gleam in Tenant's eyes, he saw that his surmise had struck home—but would his desperate plans succeed? There was not much more time; Tenant was becoming impatient. Hanley knew he would have to work fast.

Tenant was filling a hypodermic from a thin flask he had taken from his pocket. The precious moments were slipping away fast. Frantically he raked his wrists with those terrible claws. The blood was spurting from his torn veins—but the ropes were giving, were loosening, and falling away.

At last his hands were free!

But Dr Tenant's keen eyes must have seen his arms snap apart; must have read the reaction of his liberated muscles. Halfway to him with the hypodermic, the physician stopped and backed away warily, called on his dogs for help.

"No guns! No claws!" He cautioned. "I want him unharmed!"

But Hanley had other ideas about that. He heaved himself upright as the first of the charging thugs reached him, heaved himself upright and drove his fist into the fellow's face as he came up—to send the hoodlum sprawling on the floor on top of Mona Kenyon's body. The second backed away barely in time to miss the slashing claws that Hanley whipped at his throat. Momentarily the three huddled together—but they were not looking at Hanley; they were staring at the fellow on the floor—the fellow who was wallowing in Mona Kenyon's blood.

And in that moment the last of their self control snapped. Like the ravenous beasts Arthur Tenant had made of them, they threw themselves horribly upon her body....

In vain Tenant shouted orders at them. They ignored him, his power over them momentarily broken. Seething with rage he whipped out his gun and poured shots point-blank into them—but even that could not deter them. With a curse, he leaped past them—and Hanley prepared desperately to meet the onslaught.

Arms sheltering his head, he tried to ward off the savage blows that rained upon him. His steel claws were useless now. Tenant's gun barrel batted them out of the way and clubbed down on his arms, his shoulders, his skull. Punishing, bone-smashing blows! Hanley's head was ringing, his senses were swooning. Blood was streaming down into his eyes, blinding him—when a bitter curse brought hope surging back into him.

Thank God! He had not yelled and roared his accusations in vain. His plan had succeeded! Harvey Garrison had heard—and understood! The call had reached down to the manhood Arthur Tenant had not been able to snap out of him entirely!

Tenant whirled with a snarl. His gun roared once, and then again. But Garrison was too close. He hurled his falling body upon the Doctor who had betrayed him—and at last Tenant's skinny throat came within reach of the terrible glove on Jim Hanley's hand. At last those terrible claws sank deep, deep, and held their bulldog grip until the fiend who had devised them was dead....

"I never knew—I never suspected him," Harvey Garrison muttered weakly as Hanley and Connie Stewart bent over him. "He was treating me—told me I needed recreation—took me to the Dracula. He introduced me to Savold—and after that, I hardly know what happened. They must have hypnotized me. I watched that Dracula performance, and when Savold told me to play the part, I knew just what to do. My teeth sank into the girl's throat of their own accord—and after that I was lost. After that, I craved the taste of blood—so much that I turned over to them everything I own for the privilege of playing the part again tonight—and 'marrying' the victim. I was helpless, Hanley. So helpless that I had to kill my Ann—Ann Brinley—when she was only trying to save me. Oh, and, my poor—"

So that was why Ann Brinley's lips had been sealed… That was why he had failed to plumb the hell he had glimpsed in her eyes….

Jim Hanley's grey eyes were soft when he rose from beside the still figure, and the arm that encircled Connie's waist was gentle—for he had just learned a new how infinitely precious is the love of a woman.

Dracula's Brides originally appeared in *Horror Stories Magazine*, February, 1941

Wayne Rogers was born Archibald Bittner in 1897. Under his given name he edited *The Argosy* from 1928 to 1931. Under his Rogers pseudonym he had a significant pulp output including many lead stories for *The Spider* and *Operator #5* for Popular Publications.

The Solicitor:
Unnecessary Companion Letters for Chapters Two Through Four of a Perfectly Splendid Epistolary Novel by Bram Stoker

By Jamie Flanagan

Letter, Second Bride to Count

6th May

Dearest husband, noble Voivode Solomonari, Singer of the Song Sanguine, Author of the Heretical Rite, and Count Dominus,—

We write to inquire about the guest currently under our roof and your employ. A question of growing import between we three adored may only be satisfied by your wisdom, judgement, and prudence.

Regarding your solicitor, Mister Jonathan Harker—

May we eat him?

With dutiful love and eternal adoration,
SECOND, ON BEHALF OF ALL

Letter, Count to Brides

7th May

My dearest Brides,—

Mister Harker and I are currently engaged in a variety of business matters related to his talents as a solicitor and his informal role as English tutor.

With regrets deeper than I can express, we must practice restraint.

Yours forever in death,
V

Letter, Second Bride to Count

8th May

Dearest husband, Dread Warrior, Impaler of Armies, Master of Profane Arts, Bane of Gods,—

Please?

With love,
SECOND, ON BEHALF OF ALL

Letter, Count to Brides

9th May

My dear, dear Brides,—

Unfortunately, I must again deny your request. Though it pains me greatly.

With kisses for you all,
V

Letter, Second Bride to Count

10th May

Dearest Husband, Night Flyer, Blood Drinker, Animal of Battlefield and Bed, Dread Sovereign Who Needs No Instruction From Solicitors, Count of Accounts, Proficient Speaker of the English Language and Knowledgable Journeyman of European Customs,
—

We respectfully disagree.

With awe and deference,
SECOND, ON BEHALF OF ALL

Letter, Count to Brides

11th May

My Brides,—

I see what you're doing and the answer is no.

(*Unsigned*)

Letter, Second Bride to Count

13th May

To He Whom We Would Shield From the Stigma of Hypocrisy,

The assertion of the solicitor's necessity ignores years of precedent. We would direct your attention to three winters past, during which the stonework in the kitchen required a mason for mending, a necessary craftsman, whom you—in your divine judgement—chose to exsanguinate.

Left with no recourse but to proceed with the repair ourselves, we made do, though not without suffering. Third had mortar in her hair for days, which required excision by shears. It has not yet grown back, and she—as a result—remains silly in appearance. Surely you can manage the purchase of a new home abroad and book passage on a boat without counsel. Third could do that, and she's illiterate.

Sincerely,
SECOND, ON BEHALF OF ALL

P.S. 'I am not illiterate.'

THIRD, AS TRANSCRIBED BY SECOND

Letter, Count to Brides

14th May

Brides,—

The solicitor is not to be touched. I forbid it. And that's an end on it.

Definitively,
V

Letter, Count to Brides

16th May

Brides,—

Concerning our altercation yesterday evening, during which you—in defiance of my dread command—did touch, accost, and sample our guest, I wish to continue our dialogue in the interest of restoring household harmony.

I would address these matters in person would you but relent and open the chamber door.

To begin, a reminder: I am the Pater Familias, the alpha and omega. My word is sacrosanct.

Further, I request that you stop scratching at the lid of my coffin when I endeavor to rest. You'll deny having done so, but I (as one who's grappled with the Judeo-Christian God) know passive aggression when I see it.

Lastly (and this is difficult for me) I apologize if your feelings were hurt by my response to your indiscretions. I'm aware of how sensitive you three can be.

With love (as you well know),
V

P.S. I was remiss in not addressing the tragedy of Third's hair, post masonry incident. She does appear a raggle-taggle gypsy. Regrettable. Truly.

Letter, Second Bride to Count

26th June

To He Who Is Not Sorry But Shall Be,

Forgive the tardiness of this reply. Following your last missive, a lengthy discussion ensued around the topic of where to begin. We've since reached consensus, and as the first matter of business we remind you that you wouldn't know 'sorry' if it stood before you holding a sharp wooden stick.

Furthermore, your apology should include the interruption of our snack, as well as your choice to chastise us in front of the help. When the time comes to do the necessary blood letting, the three of us will scarcely be able to look Mister Harker in the eye.

In regard to your salacious accusation, we suspect the guilty party of your coffin-scratching conspiracy may or may not be the HORDE OF RATS that moved in through the aforementioned brickwork in the kitchen. (A matter we'd be eager to revisit given your keen interest in sleuthing out fault.)

Back to the Harker at hand, we find your protestations lacking. Likewise your appeals to past acts of love. I, for one, still haven't forgiven you for the murder of my first husband. And Third ever mourns Sir William Pompadour, whom you refused the dark kiss of life.

She misses him every day.

Every.

Day.

As to your artful summary of Third's appearance, that begs a question long overdue. Is she, in fact, of the Szgany? (We'll thank you not to refer to the Roma as gypsies in your reply.)

Third also asks why we're counted as opposed to named. Surely we came with a label or two?

Signed,

Three Angry Women Who Shall Remain Nameless

Letter, Count to Brides

27th June

To the Harpies barricaded in the bedchamber,—

Of course I don't know your names! I spirited you away to a world of eternal darkness and untold pleasures of flesh. Forgive me if I failed to ask, prior to the slaughter of your respective families, *'by the way, is her name Joan? She looks like a Joan.'*

The idea of naming you seemed rude, given that you doubtless had names already. In truth, I've been waiting for each of you to tell me! When I was bequeathed the dark gift, amnesia was not an associated malady. Frankly, I'm astonished that none of you remember.

If you must know, yes, two of you are Roma. One of you is high-society English. I'll let the three of you—the two with dark skin and aquiline noses, and the pale one with voluminous blonde hair—grapple with this *mystery insolutam.*

As for the fate of Sir William Pompadour, the notion of an immortal feline simply seemed wrong. (They're unsettling enough as it is.)

Good day.

V

Letter, First Bride to Vlad

28th June

Vlad,—

You'll forgive me for using your name. A rare thing, I know. As rare as a word (or letter) from me. Your first bride after death (though not before).

I take this opportunity, while the girls are at play, to write you. In doing so, I break four years of silence. It is my hope that by doing so, I ensure this message will be received with the care it deserves.

We're estranged, you and I. Distant. Quiet and unhappy. More than anything, I think the girls were born of that. For all their years, they're still young. Fast to mood, anger, flights of fancy. Sharp of tongue. Insatiable of heart.

I remember what that was like.

I remember life. And the hole that remained when you took it from me.

I raise this subject not to enflame old arguments. We've fought those battles and borne each other's curses. Distance, like pain, is a teacher. And if I've learned anything, it's that we are—and should remain—entwined. Though our bond is rooted in sickness.

To the point, I write you regarding the same cause as the girls. The solicitor. Though not for the same purpose…

I see the peasants come and go, Vlad. I see them as they prepare for a voyage. I see the box filled with earth, in which you intend to travel. I see the man—Harker—that you despise and emulate in equal measure. For his life. His love.

His Mina.

What you are about to read may be difficult to accept. Know that I write in mercy—not malice.

You cannot squeeze yourself into the confines of Mister Harker's life. Nor usurp his place within his lady's heart. Whoever Mina is, she will not replace her that you have lost. As I could not. No more than the girls could fill my emptiness, though you gifted them to me in such an effort. We're odd shapes, plucked from time, and will not fit the recesses you've carved, though you bring your weight to bear.

Kill the solicitor.

Snuff out hope.

Do not sail for unknown shores.

For the sake of the patchwork family you've crudely stitched. For the sake of those you'd uproot to add to our number. For your own sake…

You'll find no change in the voyage, save for the skies above. You seek to trade an old castle for a new manor. But this place ceased to be a castle many years ago. Now (and ever) it is your barrow. And as you stand in it now, in pain, bitterness, jealousy and melancholy, know this:

You will never leave this barrow.

May you walk from it to the wood to the wide world beyond, you will never leave this barrow. Though you travel to a far off hillside, or above mountains to a high tower, you will never leave this barrow. For the wood is the world is the hillside is the tower is the castle is the barrow. And all of these are one in you.

Stay.

For the false hope you'd spare yourself. You never loved. Never love. And will never.

Stay to bear our disdain, which—though bitter—bears virtue in honesty.

Know that if you sail for England, these will be the last words from me. Should you spread our disease, the last thread of our discourse will be cut. And when you return in failure (and you will fail) I will be motionless as a statue. I will forgo the illusions of life you've insisted upon. Be they large as dancing, or small as breath or blink. Be they soft as joy, or sharp as anger.

I will be the husk you made me. Sans artifice. A reminder of the legacy you've forged.

The girls, at want of me, will drift. Until they too recognize their tedious performances. At present, they don't realize they're pretending. Would you rob them of that innocence?

You ask our names. The girls don't remember. Chalk it up to the trauma of rebirth. Mine, I've kept, and never lost. You fancy yourself a monster, but I knew others before you, cloaked in wealth and privilege. You fancy yourself a soldier, but when you stole me, my skin was thick with battle's scars.

Why have I kept my name from you? Because names are honest things. Held by the wise, gifted by the foolish. Or sacrificed to underline a point.

May my sacrifice have meaning. May it echo in your mind.

Stay…

What remains,
ADELINE

Letter, Vlad to First Bride
(unsigned, unsealed, unsent)

~~To my treasured First Bride~~
~~To She Who Knows Me Best~~

~~To One I Stole~~
~~To What Remains of~~
Adeline,
    ~~It is pleasure, at long last—~~
    ~~How dare you? To withhold so long—~~
    For decades, I dreamt your name, only to lose it upon waking.
    To receive it now in scorn…
    ~~To think…there remained in me a final hope to break…~~

A WEATHERED JOURNAL

(Kept in shorthand, Found in the Wreckage of the Demeter)

30 June, morning. - Today, I sail for England.

VOIVODE VLAD III DRACULA OF WALLACHIA

Jamie Flanagan is a Bram Stoker Awards®–winning author. Screenwriting credits include Netflix's *The Haunting of Bly Manor*, *Midnight Mass*, *The Midnight Club*, *The Fall of the House of Usher*, AMC Shudder's *Creepshow*, and Peacock's *Hysteria*. Their short fiction and essays have appeared in anthologies and magazines such as *The Darkest Night* (ed. Lindy Ryan), *Shadows in the Stacks* (ed. Vincent V. Cava, James Sabata, and Jared Sage), *Bestiary of Blood: Modern Fables & Dark Tales* (ed. Jamal Hodge), and *Nightmare Magazine*.

Brides
By Michael R. Colangelo

"One of those big bats that they call vampires had got her in the night, and what with his gorge and the vein left open, there weren't enough blood in her to let her stand up, and I had to put a bullet through her as she lay."
—Quincey Morris, Dracula

Outside your tent, the men start hollering so loud that it startles you to life. You are up in a flash. You step out into the cold air wearing only your boots and long underwear. You brandish your bowie knife. You are prepared to use it on whatever hell awaits.

The camp is in disarray. Half-dressed cowboys run about, this way and that. The first point of panic is a fire from a broken kerosene lantern that is spreading into bedrolls, personal belongings, and ammo supplies.

The second point of panic is that all of the horses are dead. Slaughtered.

At sundown you'd placed all the horses into a little field bordered by the ruin of an old wooden fence. There is a creek, and from where you'd camped on the hill you could keep an eye on things.

Well, someone has dropped the ball, because now that field is strewn with the corpses of horses from one side all the way to the other.

Somebody shouts: "Stump, come help put this out!" But you ignore the fire and make your way down the short hillside and into the field.

The animals have been butchered. Their flesh rent and their limbs broken. Men wouldn't have the strength for this level of slaughter. Beasts have done this. Or perhaps just one very large beast.

When you go back up the hill the others have the fire under control more or less. Pierce approaches you. You ask your number two who was supposed to be on lookout.

"Bryce and Hawk, sir. Thing is, they're both missing—can't find them anywhere."

You've had men abandon you before. Sometimes it's betrayal and sometimes they'd steal from the camp before slipping away into the dark. Sometimes they'd even cut the throat of another man they didn't like on their way out. But you've never had a mutineer set fire to the place and kill all the horses before making an exit. It seems… melodramatic.

"Nobody saw anything?"

Pierce shrugs.

Someone hollers that they've found something at the tree-line. You and Pierce go investigate. It's Bryce. He's lying dead at the foot of some trees. Just like the horses, he's been slaughtered; his belly torn open wide. There are drag marks in the long grass and blood stains across the ground. It looks like something has mauled him in camp and then pulled him into the brush. There's no sign of the other man, Hawk.

"This is animals," Pierce decides. "No way some Indians or Mexicans could manage this."

"Bigfoots," you suggest. "Maybe a whole family of them."

"It's no goddamn Bigfoots," asserts Pierce.

Of course not. There's no such thing.

What to do?

You'll press on by foot. Not much else to be done. You tell Pierce to double the night watch. You tell Pierce that you all need to clean up and head out.

The camp comes slowly back under order. The mess made by the fire and confusion is cleaned up and your men bury all of the horses. They put Bryce in the ground at the end of the row. And they even have a little service for the dead man. Nobody remembers the words to the Lord's Prayer, including yourself.

The work has cost you the full day. You have no choice now but to spend the night camped on the same hill. You double the watch and put four men up instead of two. When it gets dark enough outside, you go for a walk.

The way you figure it, if something that was big or dangerous enough to kill all the horses overnight is here, then you'll find some evidence of it just by having a quick look around. As badly as you'd like to form a posse and go hunting for it properly, sometimes sneaking about has its advantages, as you've learned.

But the landscape here seems quiet enough. There are only the trickling sounds of water from the creek. You find no trails or tracks that seem out of place.

If you're lucky, whatever has caused such destruction is gone now, moved on to new hunting grounds. Or maybe there wasn't anything out here in the first place. Maybe the horses and Bryce were killed by some kind of phenomena, like space dust from the skies or invisible rays that traveled through the atmosphere.

It's starting to get cold. Darker. You decide to turn back.

You're cresting a little hill when your boot scuffs against something hard just below the topsoil. It's a flat, square stone like a mason might fashion for a cobblestone road in a town. Sure enough, as you sweep away the forest floor, you find a whole bunch more laid out and interlocking into a broken, haphazard path.

The stonework looks old. As far as you know, there isn't anything supposed to be built out here between Casper and Fort Collins. Both are leagues away from this place.

It's a mystery that immediately gets the better of you. Instead of returning to camp where it's safe, you follow the pathway.

The secret pathway takes you to a mound. It isn't a natural hill. The forest has grown all over the stone ruin to a point where if you didn't know better you might walk right overtop of it like it wasn't there at all.

You walk around the base of the hill until you find a way inside. There's a narrow gap in the earth held open by the stone framework of the ruin. It's a dark, narrow slit only wide enough to fit a man. A slim man, at that.

You've been relying on the moonlight up until now. You didn't consider bringing a lantern with you. You don't know what's in that crack, only that it's hopelessly, hopelessly dark in there.

Its probably full of snakes and spiders. At best, you'll get a nasty bite for your troubles. No thanks. You turn to go. You'd prefer to leave certain mysteries hidden to time. Then a voice calls out to you from the crack in the mound. You pause and turn back around.

It's Hawk's voice. The missing man. But how exactly Hawk got himself from the camp to being stuck in this dark hole in the ground, you don't quite know. But here you both are now.

At least you think you heard Hawk calling to you. Maybe you're tired and maybe you're stressed. Maybe or maybe not.

You reach out and put your arm into the hole. You feel around. You go as far as you can without squeezing your whole body inside.

But there's nothing in there, just more space and a bare stone wall wet to the touch. Nothing. Maybe you could come back in the morning to take another look but you doubt the others would want to waste any time.

There's a woman standing in your way. It's a blonde, middle-aged woman dressed like she's attending the plantation ball. You blink. Another hallucination. But the woman remains.

"Quincey?" she asks.

There's no time to introduce yourself. No time to explain you're Stump and not this Quincey. No time to process what this woman is doing out here in the woods, in the middle of nowhere. Because she hisses like a snake, pulls you by the lapels, presses her body forward and, with an unnatural strength, pushes you back toward the crack in the mound.

There's something wrong with her mouth. Her teeth.

You snap to your senses and understand she's no trick of the eyes. You go for the knife in your boot but it only throws your overweight body off-balance. You tip over and fall into the void. The mound sucks you inside.

The interior of the mound is as black as you thought it might be. The only bearing you are given is a weak sliver of moonlight that filters through the crack you fell through.

She's out there. She's out there waiting for you to emerge from the hole. She's sitting there like a teenager with a .22 waiting for a woodchuck to pop its head up so it can be blown off.

You feel about on the ground. Old wood and dead leaves make for good kindling. If you build a fire near the crack the smoke will be sucked right outside. You make a little pyramid out of the detritus and set it alight with your flint.

You get a weak fire going. Now there's enough warmth not to kill you overnight.

Now there's enough light to look around.

It's impossible. But there are two women down here with you. They have dark hair unlike the blonde. They look younger than she did too. They're all dressed the same though; both look like whores off a Mississippi gambling boat.

Hawk is down here too. All of his clothes are off and discarded in a torn pile nearby. He's lying in an old stone basin looking like something a medieval king might take a bath in.

Except this tub is filling up with blood, not water. Hawk's bleeding from dozens of bite wounds all over his body. He doesn't seem too bothered by it. He focuses glassy, unsteady eyes on you and smiles like a friendly drunk. And judging what's between his legs, Hawk's happy to see you, it seems.

The ladies aren't too happy to see you, though. They hiss and retreat from your firelight into the shadowy corners of the gloom. You get your knife and approach the basin.

Hawk's a real mess. Bite marks. Teeth applied to flesh with such pinpoint accuracy they've tore open all of his big veins. And it looks like he's been bleeding out for a while. Bite wounds in all the places that you never want to get bit.

The women are coming back. One on each of your flanks. When they get too close you slash out with the bowie in a horizontal arc. They pause just long enough to avoid the edge of the blade and then both hop onto you.

The dull gleam of red-stained teeth by firelight. You feel a mouth nuzzle against your neck. You feel the soft brush of lips on your throat and then the hard sharpness of a fang scrape against the skin.

You're dizzy. Senses overwhelmed with the heady scent of perfume. Your loins stir in bizarre juxtaposition to this assault. The knife is freed from your hand and flung away into the shadows. You feel teeth bite into the thin skin under your wrist and tear away the flesh. The gnawing at your neck grows more urgent and now they are both eating you alive.

Then its all over. The pair's weight lifts off you and the blonde woman from outside is standing over you. She's barking in a harsh, foreign language. The pair hiss back and there is the sound of a hollow slap as a delicate hand strikes hard across a pale, pretty face. It reminds you of starving camp dogs fighting over a piece of offal.

You take the opportunity to roll over and scurry away on hands and knees. You get to the mound's opening and squeeze your bulk back through the hole.

Outside, the sun is starting to rise. The sky's a paler shade of dark than it was before. The cold air snaps you from your hazy dream. The wound on your wrist burns terribly. You're bleeding all over yourself.

You clamp an uninjured hand over your wrist and stumble away from the mound back towards the camp. By the time you arrive, your arm is very cold. You're met by one of the lookouts.

The men sit you down in front of the campfire. They give you strong liquor to drink and bandage the wound on your wrist. You can't quite bring yourself to say what has happened. You're still trying to process it yourself.

Pierce approaches. He crouches down. "What's the next move, then?"

"We gotta move out," you say. "We're losing money out here. Bleeding it away, even."

But even as you're talking, you're still thinking about those women. And you know that now that they're on your mind they will never go away. Those teeth will haunt you if you turn away and carry on with your day-to-day.

"But look, Pierce," you add. "You and I are going to hang back and take care of something. Some nasty business."

And then you tell Pierce about what's happened. You don't spare any detail. The whole story sounds crazy as it comes from your mouth. You almost feel ashamed to say such things out loud.

The expression on Pierce's face tells you that he doesn't believe a word of it. Maybe he thinks you've lost too much blood. Maybe he thinks you're suffering some manner of trail fever.

Whatever the case, there's a reason that Pierce is your number two. That's because he never says no whether he thinks you're right or wrong.

So, with all of that put away, Pierce helps the others pack up the camp and sends them down the trail toward Casper. He stays behind to help you with your fever dream.

You return to the hidden mound with Pierce. This time, you bring a lantern with you.

Near the entrance to the place, you find Hawk dead. The women have finished him off. They've eaten his eyes and his tongue and flung him into the upper branches of an old pine. The corpse is too high up for you to pull it back down. And so you leave Hawk to the sky gods and stumble through the Lord's Prayer once again.

Inside the mound, Pierce lights the lantern and you find the women near the back of the structure. The trio are lined in a row laying in upright stone sarcophagi. They aren't dead. They aren't asleep. Their expressions are slack. Hibernation. No less weird than anything else about them.

Pierce lets out a low whistle. His eyes are wide. You can tell he's a little bit awestruck; a little bit afeared. "What do we do now, Stump?"

"We kill 'em."

You get your knife out. Approach one of the women with dark hair; the little one.

You try not to look into those vacant, empty eyes when the knife goes in. You put the blade just below her breasts where the breastbone begins and cut down through the soft parts of her torso.

It's tough cutting, too. It feels like you're trying to saw through a hunk of frozen beef. Still, you get the job done. And when you pull the knife free, you watch her colorless guts bulge and push out through the gaping wound. There isn't a trace of blood inside her.

You're about to do the next one when Pierce hollers behind you. Distracted. And now all three are on you. Snapped to life like pretty marionettes. Fingernails rake across your face like razors and draw blood into your eyes.

Now you fight. And with blood in your eyes, there's nothing hypnotic about them anymore. They're faster and a little bit stronger than you are, but you're of hefty weight and good in a knife fight; handy with a blade.

And even though you are winning your end of the fight, you can hear that Pierce is not winning his end. The man is screaming and they are eating him to death. There is no time to worry about it.

You fight until there is nothing left to fight. Your blind swings connect with nothing. Everything is quiet. You pause.

The trio is standing over the jigsaw body of Pierce. Your number two has been reduced to a bloody, whimpering pile of flesh.

The blonde turns and flashes you a wry smile: "Quincey?"

"I ain't Quincey," you say. You wipe the blood from your face and find there is only more blood there.

A strong, cold hand wraps about your throat. It cuts off your angry words. Your ability to breathe is gone. You feel teeth on your neck. Your blood flows as a vein tears loose.

The knife is snatched from your hand and placed firmly in your groin. The trio topple you over. You have no strength left to resist them any longer.

The blonde is eye-to-eye with you now, she smiles again. Her eyes are full of sex. She knows you are finished too.

"Quincey," she whispers to you like she's been reunited with an old lover.

Then she takes the tongue from your head, gouges out both of your eyes.

And there's nothing left for you down here but the sensations of old teeth.

Michael R. Colangelo is a writer from Toronto, but was raised in Whitby (Ontario, Canada). He has published numerous short stories and edited for numerous publications. In 2012, he was awarded the Richard Laymon President's Award for Service by the Horror Writers Association for his work within the organization. Visit him at: michaelrcolangelo.blogspot.com.